### "I've heard tell of a young man who is travelling around the country killing people."

"Killing people? How do you mean?"

"He's been backing men into a corner until their only recourse is to draw on him. The way I hear it, none of them have even gotten their guns out of their holster."

"So the kid's fast," the Gunsmith said. "Why tell me?"

"He says his name is John Adams."

"I don't know the name," Clint replied.

"He goes around telling people that he's your son . . ."

Don't miss any of the lusty, hard-riding action in the
Charter Western series, THE GUNSMITH:

1. MACKLIN'S WOMEN
2. THE CHINESE GUNMEN
3. THE WOMAN HUNT
4. THE GUNS OF ABILENE
5. THREE GUNS FOR GLORY
6. LEADTOWN
7. THE LONGHORN WAR
8. QUANAH'S REVENGE
9. HEAVYWEIGHT GUN
10. NEW ORLEANS FIRE
11. ONE-HANDED GUN
12. THE CANADIAN PAYROLL
13. DRAW TO AN INSIDE DEATH
14. DEAD MAN'S HAND
15. BANDIT GOLD
16. BUCKSKINS AND SIX-GUNS
17. SILVER WAR
18. HIGH NOON AT LANCASTER
19. BANDIDO BLOOD
20. THE DODGE CITY GANG

21. SASQUATCH HUNT
22. BULLETS AND BALLOTS
23. THE RIVERBOAT GANG
24. KILLER GRIZZLY
25. NORTH OF THE BORDER
26. EAGLE'S GAP
27. CHINATOWN HELL
28. THE PANHANDLE SEARCH
29. WILDCAT ROUNDUP
30. THE PONDEROSA WAR
31. TROUBLE RIDES A FAST HORSE
32. DYNAMITE JUSTICE
33. THE POSSE
34. NIGHT OF THE GILA
35. THE BOUNTY WOMEN
36. BLACK PEARL SALOON
37. GUNDOWN IN PARADISE
38. KING OF THE BORDER
39. THE EL PASO SALT WAR
40. THE TEN PINES KILLER

And coming next month:
THE GUNSMITH #42: THE WYOMING CATTLE KILL

## HELL WITH A PISTOL

J. R. ROBERTS

CHARTER BOOKS, NEW YORK

To
Mike and Kathy M.

THE GUNSMITH #41: HELL WITH A PISTOL

A Charter Book/published by arrangement with
the author

PRINTING HISTORY
Charter Original/June 1985

All rights reserved.
Copyright © 1985 by Robert J. Randisi
This book may not be reproduced in whole
or in part, by mimeograph or any other means,
without permission. For information address:
The Berkley Publishing Group, 200 Madison Avenue,
New York, New York 10016.

ISBN: 0-441-30942-9

Charter Books are published by The Berkley Publishing Group,
200 Madison Avenue, New York, New York 10016.
PRINTED IN THE UNITED STATES OF AMERICA

# ONE

There was nothing remarkable about the young man as he entered the Perryville Saloon, nothing that would draw the eye to him. Oh, he wore a gun, but there was nothing unusual about that. He was tall and slim, looking younger than his eighteen years, and no one gave him a second glance.

The saloon was crowded, and in some places, bodies were stacked two deep at the bar. The young man made his way to the bar and appeared to be waiting patiently for an opportunity to order a drink.

Finally, a space opened. The young man spotted it, but so did another, larger man. To anyone who might have been watching, it seemed as if the young man was in a better position to claim the opening, yet he seemed to wait. As the larger man moved to fill it, the slighter man moved with him, and contact was made.

"Watch who you're pushing," the younger man yelled out, giving the larger man a shove with both hands.

The bigger man was pushed off balance and fell against two other men.

"Hey, watch it!" he shouted at the young man.

The young man had moved into the opening at the bar and was ignoring the other man. This did not sit well with him, so he placed a large hand on the young man's shoulder and pulled him around to face him. By this time, the young man had a beer in his hand, and as he spun around, he emptied the contents on the bigger man's chest.

"Goddamn you!" the man bawled.

"Get away from me!" the young man shouted back, pushing the man again. The big man took two backward steps before setting himself.

"I'm gonna thrash you, boy, and teach you some manners," he said.

"I won't fight with you," the young man said as all other activity in the saloon settled down. A fight was in the offing, and that always took precedence over the more mundane matters of gambling and drinking.

"You won't have to," the other man said. "I'll just put you over my knee, boy."

"If you take a move toward me," the boy said, holding out his left hand and allowing his right to hover near his gun, "I'll have to kill you."

The big man looked surprised and placed both hands on his hips.

"What did you say?"

"Boy said he was gonna kill you, Les," another man said from the bar.

"That's what I thought he said, Ben, but I just didn't believe my ears." The man looked at the boy and said, "You sure you can heft that great big gun, boy?"

"You just try me," the young man said confidently.

"I think I'll give you a whipping instead," the man called Les said, taking one step towards him.

"Another step and I'll have to shoot you."

"Boy, you're just asking for trouble you don't need."

"Either draw your gun or leave, mister."

"Oh, I ain't leaving, sonny," the man said. "You are—feet first."

No one in the saloon noticed the satisfied look that crept into the young man's eyes as he realized that the other man was finally going to draw.

"Your name is Les?" he asked.

"That's right."

"Les what?"

"You interested in the name of the man who's gonna kill you, boy?"

"I'm interested in the name of the man I'm going to kill."

"My name's Les Whitely, boy. What's your name?"

"My name is Adams," the young man said, "John Adams. That name mean anything to you?"

"Not a thing?"

"Nothing."

"The name Adams doesn't sound familiar?"

"I heard of Clint Adams," a man at the bar said, laughing into his beer. "But you ain't him."

"No, I'm not," the young man said, happy that someone had brought up the name. "I'm his son."

"You're the Gunsmith's kid?" the man at the bar asked with genuine interest.

"That's right."

"You're gonna kill the son of a legend, Les," the man said, and it was plain in his tone that he was glad he was not in that situation himself.

"That's the legend's rough luck," Les said, puffing out his chest. "He got hisself a son with a big mouth, and now they're both gonna have to pay the price."

Looking at Adams Les Whitely said, "You ready, boy?"

"Whenever you are, Mr. Whitely," the young man said with a note of false respect.

"Too late to try and get on my good side, boy—" Whitely said, and went for his gun.

The man was slow, and only the youth of his opponent had given him any degree of confidence. John Adams drew his own gun and shot the man squarely in the chest before he even had a chance to touch his weapon.

He holstered his gun, and turning his back, walked from the saloon without even watching the man fall.

This time it had been too easy.

"How come nobody called me while this young gunslick was still here?" the sheriff of Perryville, Colorado, demanded, as he watched the dead man being carried from the saloon. His name was Horace Greenfield, and at better than fifty, he was over-the-hill for a lawman and was secretly satisfied that no one *had* called him while the young gunman had still been there.

"He was here and gone so fast, Sheriff," the man called Ben replied. "It was like he came here just to shoot ol' Les."

"What did this fella look like?" the lawman asked.

Men exchanged glances and many of them shrugged.

"He was young," Ben said, looking around for help.

"Hell, and he was fast," another man offered.

"Yeah, real fast," a third chimed in.

"You suppose he really was who he said he was?" Ben asked the crowd.

"And just who was that?" Sheriff Horace Greenfield asked.

Ben turned back to the sheriff and answered, "He said his name was Adams, John Adams."

"So?"

"He claimed his daddy was Clint Adams," Ben said. "He said he was the Gunsmith's son."

# TWO

"I'd still like to know how you found your way here to Labyrinth, Texas, Mary," Clint Adams said to the woman in bed with him.

"Can we talk about that . . . later?" she asked, wrapping her arms around his neck and drawing him down to her waiting mouth.

He was about to answer, but his words would have been lost inside her mouth, so instead he accepted her darting tongue as it sought out his own.

Clint had met Mary Randall just months ago in El Paso, Texas, when he had become involved in what he had come to call the El Paso Salt War.[1] The young woman, who was petite in every aspect but her powerful thighs and boundless energy, had interested him immediately, and the feeling had been reciprocated. He had been shocked to see her come riding into Labyrinth just that morning, and still had not been able to get an explanation from her as to whether or not her appearance was planned or a coincidence.

---

[1] Gunsmith #39: The El Paso Salt War

She climbed on top of him and squatted, took Clint's rock hard length inside of her and began to ride him up and down. It had been a favorite position for them during his time in El Paso, and as he had done then, he ran his hands over her thighs, enjoying the play of her incredible muscles beneath the surface.

As much as they enjoyed each other, he knew that it could not have been this that brought her here to Labyrinth. Had he mentioned Labyrinth to her during his stay in El Paso? He couldn't recall. The town had become sort of an unofficial headquarters for him, and the fact that he never stayed for very long stretches of time suited the town law just fine. As long as there was no trouble, Sheriff Nat Gooden was satisfied to tolerate his occasional visits.

Gooden and Clint Adams spoke very infrequently. Clint's friend, Rick Hartman, put it down to jealousy.

As Mary continued to ride Clint up and down, sliding her hot, soaking chasm up and down his throbbing shaft, all other thoughts fled from his mind, and he became aware only of her and the pleasure she was giving him. Of course, she was receiving as good as she got, as evidenced by the fact that her head was thrown back, her eyes were tightly closed, and her breath was coming in deep gasps.

Suddenly she came down on him and stayed down, grinding her crotch tightly against his. He could feel her spasms as her hungry pussy sucked at him. He couldn't stand very much of that before he was spurting inside of her, giving her all she could handle and more. His own grunts of pleasure mingled with her cries and moans, and then she collapsed on top of him in a supine position, her breath hot on his neck.

"That was quite a hello," he said, and she giggled against his chest.

She had not even had time to get a hotel room. When they had spotted each other, she'd dismounted from her horse, thrown her arms around his neck, and they'd gone straight to his hotel room.

"If you remember," she said, "we had quite a goodbye, as well."

"Oh, I remember," he said. Their goodbye had been shared with another young woman, Sally Fountain, whose idea it had been for the three of them to share a bed—and it had turned out to be an excellent one.

"As much as I like Sally, though," Mary said, snuggling up to him, "I'm glad I've got you all to myself right now."

"So am I," he said. It had been hard for him to choose a favorite between the two girls, but soon after he had left El Paso he found himself thinking more of little Mary than tall and lean Sally.

"I'm glad to hear that," she said.

"How is Sally?"

"Last time I saw her she was fine. Her father's retired, and she's looking after him."

"Good," he said. "Now what about you?"

"What about me?"

"What brings you to Labyrinth?"

"I was just riding through," she said. "I got tired of El Paso after you left."

"Did you know I was here?"

She hesitated before answering, then said, "You never mentioned it, but as I was travelling through Texas I heard tell that you might be here. Is this some sort of home base for you?"

"It's become that, yeah," he said. "I usually stop here when I'm in the vicinity."

"Well, I'm glad you were here when I came in."

"Where are you headed?"

"I don't know really. Do they need someone with my talents here?"

Mary was a saloon girl when Clint met her in El Paso.

"I have a friend name of Rick Hartman who owns the best saloon in town—if you're interested, I can speak to him."

"Do you have any objections?"

Clint had always shied away from forming attachments with any women in Labyrinth, but he found that he had no objections to Mary possibly getting a job there.

"No, I wouldn't mind at all."

"I'm glad," she said, hugging him tightly.

To his surprise the Gunsmith said, "So am I."

"Is she . . . a friend of yours?" Rick Hartman asked the Gunsmith.

"Yes. We met in El Paso."

"And she followed you here?"

"No, she just left El Paso and ended up here."

"You believe that?" Rick asked. He was a tall, slender man about Clint's age, and they had been friends ever since he had saved Clint Adams from a life in the bottle following Bill Hickok's death.

"Yes."

"You didn't make this girl any promises while you were in El Paso, did you?" Rick asked with an amused

# HELL WITH A PISTOL

look. He was aware of his friend's fondness for the opposite sex and of their near obsession with him.

"You know me better than that."

"Yes, but I thought I knew you better than this, too," Rick replied. "You really want me to give this girl a job?"

"She's a nice young woman, Rick," Clint said, "and she needs a job."

"Will she work *hard?*" Rick asked. He was asking if Mary would go upstairs with a man if the man offered to pay enough.

"That would be up to you."

"You know I don't make my girls work that way, Clint," Rick said. "It's up to them."

"Fine."

"All right, then," Rick Hartman said with a sigh. "Tell her she can start tomorrow."

"Don't you want to take a look at her?"

Rick smiled broadly and said, "Oh, I trust your taste, Clint."

"You bastard," Clint said with genuine affection.

Rick Hartman's face suddenly went serious and he said, "Now let's discuss something else."

"What? My bar bill? You know I always pay—"

"No, damn it, not your bar bill. *You* know I always eat *that*."

"I keep telling you I'll pay."

"And I keep telling you that you don't pay in my place—for anything."

"Okay, okay, then what do you want to discuss?"

Hartman's face was more serious than Clint could remember having seen it in some time.

"There are some rumors going around, Clint, which

I'm sure you haven't heard."

"What makes you so sure."

"Because if you had heard you wouldn't be here right now, you'd be on the trail checking it out."

Now Clint was interested.

"What kind of rumors are we talking about?"

"I've heard tell of a young man who is travelling around the country killing people."

"Killing people? How do you mean?"

"I mean he's been backing men into a corner until their only recourse is to draw on him."

"And he kills them?"

"The way I hear it, none of them have even gotten their gun out of their holster."

"So the kid's fast," Clint said. "Why tell me?"

"The kid's name . . ." Rick began, and then trailed off as if he didn't quite know how to say what he had to say.

"Yeah? What's the kid's name?"

"He says that his name is John Adams."

"John Adams," Clint repeated. "I don't know the name, Rick. Why are you telling me all this?"

"He's got the same last name as you, Clint."

"So? There are lots of people named Adams. What's your point? You're not saying I ought to track this kid down and put a stop to what he's doing just because we have the same last name, are you? I'm not in the law business anymore, Rick. You know that."

"I know that. There's something else though. . ."

"What the hell is wrong with you? Do I have to drag it out of you?"

"The kid says . . . ah shit, he says he's your son, Clint."

"What?" Clint asked, not sure he'd heard right.
"He goes around telling people that he's the Gunsmith's son!"

# THREE

Lying in bed that night with Mary warm beside him, Clint thought about the scene that took place in Rick Hartman's office earlier in the day.

"Have you been sampling your own whiskey again?" he'd asked Hartman. "Where did you hear an incredible story like that?"

"From here and there," Rick said.

Clint marvelled at times at how many "ears" Rick Hartman seemed to have—and his information was usually good.

"I don't have a son," Clint said, rather lamely. "Hell, I don't even have any kids."

"Are you sure?"

"Don't you think I'd know a thing like that?" Clint asked, fidgeting in his chair.

"Maybe not."

"What's that supposed to mean?"

"Don't get edgy with me, Clint," Hartman said. "I

know how you like women. You've planted your seed in a lot of places over the years. How do you know it didn't take root once or twice?"

Clint had opened his mouth to reply and then abruptly shut it again.

How, indeed?

It was true that over the years the Gunsmith had not been shy with women. His luck with the fairer sex had always seemed—well, phenomenal, to say the least. He could remember incidents where he had exchanged initial glances with a woman one moment, and found himself in bed with her the next. He knew that, on occasion, it was his reputation—the name the Gunsmith—that was the cause, but he was also vain enough to think that, for the most part, women were just attracted to him, and he was certainly attracted to them.

Lying awake, virtually unable to sleep, Clint Adams began to think back eighteen years in his mind, trying to find a woman who might have given birth to a boy who would be old enough to kill by now.

How many children might he have by now?

There was a blonde girl named Sara, whose last name he had never even learned. That was when he'd had to face down Con Macklin and a private army of killers.[2]

Then there was red-haired Jenny Sand, whom he had almost married, lost, found, and lost—or let go—again thirteen years later.[3]

---

[2] *The Gunsmith #1: Macklin's Women*
[3] *The Gunsmith #3: The Woman Hunt*

# HELL WITH A PISTOL 17

In Avalon, New Mexico—a town nicknamed "Leadtown"—he had met and spent time with blonde newspaperwoman J. T. Archer.[4]

There were may others just over the past few years, since he'd given up his badge and taken to the life of a travelling gunsmith: Estralita Martinez and Laura Kennedy, two very different women he had met in Lansdale, Texas[5]; the raven-haired Michelle Bouchet, from New Orleans[6]; Carolyn Gray Fox, the dark-haired, courageous Indian woman from Nevada[7]; Lacy Blake, lady bounty hunter[8]; and Beverly Press, the lady rancher from Wyoming,[9] just to name some of the more memorable ladies from his past.

And then there was Joanna Morgan, a woman he unflinchingly admitted that he had loved and lost to devil "death" north of the border in Alaska.[10]

Those women had all been special to him. Would any of them have born a child and not tried to get in touch with him to let him know? That was entirely possible. All of those women had understood the nature of the man they had become involved with, and none of them would have wanted to try and use a child to tie him down.

Looking down at the young woman who lay contentedly in the crook of his arm, he wondered if he should seek them out and find out?

No, he told himself, first things had to come first.

---

[4] *The Gunsmith #6: Leadtown*
[5] *The Gunsmith #7: The Longhorn War*
[6] *The Gunsmith #10: New Orleans Fire*
[7] *The Gunsmith #17: Silver War*
[8] *The Gunsmith #24: Killer Grizzly*
[9] *The Gunsmith #28: The Panhandle Search*
[10] *The Gunsmith #25: North of the Border*

There was a boy—a killer, by all accounts—out there laying claim to the name Adams, and claiming to be his son. As much as Clint Adams disliked being called the Gunsmith, he disliked even more someone else trying to build a reputation on his name—even if that someone turned out to be his own son.

Finding the young man who called himself John Adams and stopping his string of killings was not even a consideration for Clint Adams. Those kinds of decisions were well behind him now. His only real concern was to find out if John Adams was really his son, or just an opportunistic young man who may think he's come up with a good way to build his reputation.

If this was the case, then the young Mr. Adams was going to find that he had picked the wrong coattails on which to try to ride to fame.

John Adams wondered where the Gunsmith was.

Sooner or later, Clint Adams would have to hear about him. What would he do? Would he come looking for him to claim him as his son, or to stop him?

He wouldn't have much chance of stopping him, that much was for sure. Young John was having himself too good a time, and was well on his way to making a name for himself. His next step was to move onto a new territory and continue to spread his own fame.

So where was the fabled Gunsmith now, and what was he thinking, John Adams wondered, as he placed his hand on the left buttock of the saloon girl whose bed he was sharing. The girl moaned and turned her head, snoring slightly.

You can't help but be curious about a father you've never met, John thought with an amused grin as he slapped the girl's buttock, abruptly waking her.

"Come on, sweet thing," he said, feeling the heat rising in his groin, "it's time for you to earn your money."

The following morning Clint went to Rick Hartman's place and woke him up too.

"Where's the last place you heard this son of mine was?" he asked.

"You woke me up to ask me that?" Rick asked, peering at Clint with sleep-laden eyes.

"Come on, Rick," Clint said. "Now that you're awake think how much fun it will be waking up your friend."

"What friend?"

"I don't know," Clint said, shrugging. "Which gal did you take to bed with you last night?"

Rick frowned, scratched his head and then said sheepishly, "Damned if I can remember. I'll have to check."

"Well, go ahead and check, but first answer my question."

"Colorado," Rick said. "Town called Perryville."

"Thanks."

"You going looking for him?"

"Yep."

"To do what?"

"To find out if he's really my son."

"Not to stop him from claiming he is?" Rick asked. "And, from killing people?"

"If he's mine, I'll stop him."

"And if he's not?"

Clint hesitated, then said, "Hell, since I'll be in the neighborhood, I might as well stop him anyway."

"That's what I thought. Be careful, huh?"

"Always."

"And don't worry about Mary," Rick said. "I'll watch over her for you."

"She can watch over herself," Clint said, grinning at his friend. "Try something, and you'll find that out."

"Oh," Rick said as Clint started to walk away, "did she find a room to stay in?"

"Yes, she did," Clint said over his shoulder. "Mine!"

# FOUR

When Clint Adams rode out of Labyrinth, his mind was filled with faces and places from the distant and not so distant past. Examining his past was something the Gunsmith was never particularly fond of doing because he usually managed to pick a time or place out of his past in which he might have avoided becoming the Gunsmith.

And, if John Adams didn't have the Gunsmith to claim as a father, maybe his life might have been different too.

The last thing he needed was another reason to hate the name the Gunsmith.

At first glance, Perryville, Colorado, was a thoroughly forgettable town.

After leaving Duke at the livery he went directly to the sheriff's office and introduced himself.

"Clint Adams!" the sheriff repeated. He stood up abruptly, knocking his chair over backward. It was obvious that Horace Greenfield recognized the name.

"That's right, Sheriff."

"Well—uh, wha-what can I do for you, Mr. Adams?" the lawman stammered.

"You can stop chattering your teeth and answer a few questions for me."

"S-sure."

It was obvious to Clint that Greenfield was one of those men who enjoyed being sheriff as long as they never had to earn the title. He had no use for men like that. If he knew he didn't have the backbone to do the job right, he shouldn't have taken it.

"A couple of weeks ago there was a killing here."

"A killing?" Greenfield said nervously. He was a stocky, out-of-condition man over fifty. It was becoming increasingly hard for Clint to remain in the same room with him without showing his contempt for the man.

"I'm sure you remember it."

"Oh, yeah, sure," Greenfield said, righting his chair but not sitting in it. "I remember."

"Greenfield, sit down," Clint said in disgust.

"Yessir," the pathetic lawman said, obeying the Gunsmith immediately.

Clint leaned on the desk with both hands and said, "Now, I'm not going to be in your town long, *Sheriff*," making the title sound like a dirty word. "I find Perryville uninspiring, and I find that you fit right in as sheriff. All I want to do is get some answers and get the hell out. Is that clear enough for you?"

Greenfield's teeth started chattering again.

After leaving Greenfield's office Clint went to the saloon where the shooting had taken place. During the course of the day he talked with many of the men who were present at the shooting. The description of the actual incident was the same as Rick had described—it had seemed as if the kid wanted the other man to draw.

When Clint left Perryville, Colorado, all he knew was that John Adams killed a man and left town immediately after. Nobody knew which way he went, and nobody cared.

The trail was cold—but a cold trail was better than no trail.

"Drift, Duke," he said, and gave the big black his head to leave town any way he wanted to. The huge animal headed east.

If John Adams was actually his son, then Clint could simply trust his own instincts about which way he would go if he had just killed a man and didn't want to have to explain it to the law.

If the kid wasn't his—well, with a cold trail, one direction was as good as another. You just kept going until it started to heat up again.

# FIVE

Prosperity, New Mexico. The scene was a familiar one for John Adams. He was facing a man he had virtually backed into a corner. The man had to draw on him or be branded a coward. The game was working to perfection, as it always did—and maybe that was a problem.

The young man was tiring of the game and thought that perhaps he should go on to one with bigger stakes.

But this wasn't the time to let his mind wander. There was a man with a gun standing before him, waiting to be killed.

John Adams obliged him.

Clint was in a town called Ryan's Glen, in the southern portion of Colorado, sitting in a saloon wondering if he should send a telegram to Rick Hartman to see if his friend had heard anything, when someone told him a story about a gunfight in New Mexico. The description of the incident fit the pattern and so did the description of the man who came out of it alive.

John Adams.

He heard the story—or parts of it—as an exchange between two saddle-tramps at the next table.

"What was that you said about New Mexico?" Clint asked one of the two men.

The man who had been talking looked over at him and said, "Damnedest thing you'd ever want to see. Just a punk kid, but he had a move like lightning."

"Did you see it?"

"What?"

"Were you there, or did you just hear about it?"

"I heard tell," the man replied. "I heard tell this kid pushed a fella into drawing on him, and then never let him clear leather." He looked back at his friend then and said, "Like nothing you ever seen before."

"What town?" Clint asked.

"Huh?"

"What town I said."

"I dunno," the man said, shrugging. "New Mexico was all I heard."

"Sure," Clint said. "Thanks."

"Damnedest thing you ever . . ." the man was saying as the Gunsmith left the saloon.

John Adams had struck again—and the trail was heating up.

Following the incident in Prosperity, John Adams picked the town at Canaan, New Mexico, in which to rest. All he needed was a week or so to catch his breath and re-evaluate his position. Should he continue going on the way he was, or step up his quest for fame by going after a gunman with a big name or even a lawman?

He'd take some time, do some drinking, gambling, and whoring, and study on it.

Frank Montana was a killer.

There were gunmen, and outlaws, and hardcases, and Montana could have qualified as any of these, but put pure and simple, he was a killer. He hunted men for money, and he killed them.

Montana even looked like a killer. At thirty-five years of age, his face wore a look of perpetual boredom, and it never changed, whether he was caressing a deck of cards, a woman, or his Walker Colt.

Right now, he was on the trail of a young gunman who was out to make a name for himself and was doing a pretty good job of it.

He'd heard the stories about the shooting in New Mexico, too, and he was headed that way. This John Adams had not yet built up a big price on his head, but then he wasn't Frank Montana's primary target either. The Adams kid was claiming to be the son of Clint Adams, the Gunsmith, and Montana figured that whether the kid was telling the truth or not, his claims were sure to draw the Gunsmith to him—and Montana would be waiting. There was no price on Clint Adams he knew, but he also knew that killing the Gunsmith would enhance his already considerable reputation. Hell, and killing his fast-gun son wouldn't hurt either. In fact, it just might elevate him to the point where he would be damn near a legend.

And, a legend could name his own price.

Canaan was a small town, quiet and peaceful. He'd never been there before, but at first sight John Adams knew it was just what he was looking for. It had a saloon with some good gambling going on and a bawdy house.

He'd made the right choice.

Clint Adams left Ryan's Glen, Colorado, and headed for New Mexico, hoping that this search for the boy who claimed to be his son wouldn't take too much of his time—or too many of his bullets.

# SIX

Ron Diamond had been living in Canaan, New Mexico, for five years, only the people there knew him as Dan Rondo. If they knew who he really was, he doubted that he'd be able to continue this quiet life he'd been leading for five years.

"Dan?"

He turned and looked at his wife, who had a concerned look on her face.

Dan Rondo was forty-six, tall, and slender with slate gray hair—a feature that had not come with age. He'd had gray hair since he was twenty years old.

Delores Rondo was twenty, and they had been married for two years. Rondo had wanted her before that, but he had decided to wait until the young girl became a young woman, and eighteen seemed the right age.

"Is something wrong, my love?" she asked.

Rondo approached his lovely young Mexican wife and put his hands on her shoulders.

"Nothing's wrong, honey."

"Why do you stare out the window like that?"

He shrugged. Lately he'd been staring out the window a lot, and she'd caught him once or twice. He couldn't explain it to her. What did she know of the smell of trouble in the air?

"No reason, honey, really," he said, taking her into his powerful arms.

Delores Rondo laid her head against her husband's chest and wondered again—as she had many times before—who he was. She knew that his name was not really Rondo, but beyond that she knew nothing. All she knew for sure was that he loved her, and she loved him, and the difference in their ages had no effect on that, no matter what her father thought.

Dan Rondo hugged his wife tightly, inhaling the fragrance of her long, dark hair, feeling her large, firm breasts crushed against his chest, and again wondered how an old fool like him could have been so lucky as to have such a young and beautiful wife. She made him feel young again—and he was feeling younger than ever at the moment.

"I'll tell you what, Delores," he said. "Why don't we go in the back and try and take my mind off . . . wandering."

Smiling happily Delores said, "I think I can do that."

Rondo laughed heartily and said, "I know you can."

On the way to the back room he took one last sniff at the air and, sure enough, there was trouble brewing.

The Soble brothers were heading for Canaan because they needed a place to cool off. Sam, Ned, and

# HELL WITH A PISTOL

Charlie had hit three Texas banks over the past week and were smart enough to know that it was time to take a break.

"What do you know about this town, Canaan?" Charlie Soble asked Sam, his oldest brother, while they were breaking camp to head for the town in question.

"I know it's small and quiet, and it ain't got much law to speak of," Sam said. Sam Soble was thirty-five, the oldest of the three, and the accepted leader. Charlie was nineteen, and Ned was twenty-seven. Anyone would be able to tell that they were brothers because they had the same broad shoulders, narrow hips, and angular face as their father, old Ethan Soble.

"The perfect place to hole up, huh?" Ned asked.

"Perfect," Sam said.

"But for how long?" Charlie asked.

"Who knows?" Sam said. "I'll let you know when it's time to move again."

"Why couldn't we go to San Francisco or some place like that?" Charlie complained. "Some place where I could enjoy this money?" He touched his saddlebag, which contained ten thousand dollars, one third of their total take.

"We've split the money up, Charlie," Sam said to his little brother. "You want to go to San Francisco or some other big town, you go right ahead."

"Ned?" Charlie said.

Ned shook his head and said, "I'm staying with Sam, Charlie."

Sam and Ned mounted up, then turned and looked back at their little brother, who was thoughtfully chewing his lower lip.

"Little brother?" Sam asked.

"Yeah, yeah," Charlie Soble said, mounting up, "I'm coming."

"Be patient, Charlie," Sam said. "I'll get you to San Francisco."

"Promise, Sammy?" Charlie asked eagerly.

"I promise," Sam Soble said, "as long as you never call me Sammy again!"

John Adams was checking into the Canaan Hotel when Delores walked in. She was a beautiful, dark-haired, big-breasted Mex gal, about nineteen or twenty years old. He couldn't take his eyes off her as she exchanged some Spanish dialogue with the desk clerk. She noticed him watching her, met his eyes once and then looked away. He watched her until she disappeared up the stairs.

"Hey, who was that?" he asked the clerk, who was also a Mexican.

"Her name is Delores, Señor."

"Does she work here?"

"Sometimes she comes in and cleans rooms," the man said.

"She married?"

"Si."

"Too bad."

"Will you sign the register, please?"

"Sure."

He turned the book around and scribbled something unintelligible.

"Señor?" the man asked when he couldn't read the name.

"Leave it at that, okay?" John Adams said. "I'll tell

# HELL WITH A PISTOL

you what. You can call me Kid."

"Si, Señor . . . Kid."

"What room do I have?"

"Eh, ocho, Señor," the man said. "Room eight."

"Thanks."

Adams went up the steps, hoping that he would find the girl Delores cleaning out room eight.

The girl was just coming out of his room as he reached it. She stopped short when she saw him, hesitated, then tried to slide by him with her back against the wall. He stepped in her way in time to feel her big breasts bounce off him. They felt damned good beneath the thin fabric of her dress, firm and bouncy.

"Mmm, that feels good," he said. "How's it feel to you, Delores, sweetheart?"

She backed up quickly, breaking the contact and averting his eyes.

"Please," she whispered, "please, I am married . . ."

He stared at her, admiring her high cheekbones and dark eyes, the musky scent of her, watching as her breasts rose and fell with her rapid breathing, and he felt the familiar stirring between his legs.

"All right, Delores," he said, stepping aside. "You can go. But we'll see each other again, real soon."

She hurried down the hall so quickly that her dress swirled, flashing him a look at her solid legs, and then he went into his room, laughing. The ache between his legs could wait a while. Waiting would make it feel that much better when he took care of it.

That is, when Delores took care of it.

● ● ●

The Soble boys reached Canaan a few hours after John Adams did. While they were checking into the hotel, Adams was relaxing at the cantina over a bottle of whiskey.

"Why do we all have to squeeze into one room?" Charlie complained. "We got all this money—"

"And we want to keep it, Charlie," Ned said.

"You've got yours, Charlie," Sam told him. "Go ahead, get your own room."

"Ned?" Charlie said.

"I'm staying with Sam."

"Yeah," Charlie said, "me too."

Sam and Ned exchanged glances, and then Sam said, "Let's go get a drink."

"Or two," Ned said.

"Yeah," Charlie agreed, and they left the hotel.

Clint Adams had crossed the border from Texas into New Mexico, and by the time he rode into the town of Hardwood, he was beginning to feel the pangs of frustration. John Adams was proving to be a more elusive quarry than he had anticipated.

All of a sudden the boy seemed to have vanished from sight. Perhaps the young gunman had heard that the Gunsmith was looking for him, or maybe he had simply decided to take a rest.

Still, by last report he was in New Mexico and had to put in another appearance sooner or later. Clint didn't know the boy, but his movements to date seemed to dictate that he wouldn't stay out of circulation for very long. Men like that—killer's like that—craved notoriety.

Althought Clint knew that it was the same as waiting

for some poor soul to catch a bullet, he decided that his best move at this point would be to stay put and wait for John Adams to once again announce his location.

# SEVEN

Hardwood, New Mexico, had everything the Gunsmith would need to sustain him while waiting for a sign from John Adams. It had a hotel, a saloon which meant plenty of whiskey and gambling, and it had a café in addition to the hotel's dining room, and a telegraph office.

After putting Duke up at the livery and registering in the hotel, Clint went in search of the town sheriff to announce his arrival and his intention to stay in town a while—hopefully, a short while.

The sheriff was a tall, lanky man with huge hands whose knuckles were so large Clint wondered how he ever got to his gun without them getting in the way. The middle knuckle of the left hand was especially swollen and scraped, some indication that the sheriff solved some of the town's problems with his bare hands.

"Clint Adams, huh?" Sheriff Tom Smithson said with interest. "What brings the Gunsmith to these parts? Not much here to interest you."

"I'm looking for someone," Clint replied, "and this seems a good enough place to hole up and wait for some word on him."

"Anyone in particular?"

"Fella calling himself John Adams."

"Kin?"

"He claims to be my son."

"Guess that's a good enough reason to be looking for someone," the sheriff said. "You got peaceable intentions?"

"Sheriff, in spite of my reputation, I always have peaceable intentions."

"Seems to me I've heard that about you once or twice," the man said, nodding. "All right, Mr. Adams. I don't have any objection to your staying in Hardwood a spell, long as you don't cause any trouble."

"Guess I can't rightly promise not to cause any, Sheriff," Clint said, "but I can sure as hell promise not to *start* any."

The sheriff thought about that a few moments, then nodded shortly and said, "Fair enough."

"Reckon I'll go over and give the saloon a try," Clint said, then. "If you find the time, I'd be honored if you'd have a drink with me later."

"I think I'll be able to find the time," the sheriff said readily. "Much obliged."

"See you later, then," Clint said and left the man's office. The sheriff had impressed him as a no-nonsense, confident man, and he liked that. He hoped the man would take him up on his offer of a drink after all.

Clint had gotten himself involved in a poker game by

the time the sheriff arrived for that drink. He had already alerted the bartender, a florid-faced, big-bellied man called "Windy," that the lawman might be along to join him for a drink, and he nodded to the man as Smithson entered. By the time the sheriff reached the bar, his beer was waiting for him. He picked it up, raised it towards Clint and sipped it.

He took the beer and approached the table to watch the game's progress. After a few hands Clint was even and decided to quit. His luck had been bad, but he was a good enough player not to have lost during the bad streak.

"Another drink?" he asked the sheriff as he stood up.

"Sure."

At the bar, after they each had a beer in hand, the lawman said, "You're a good poker player. You had some bad hands there, but managed to avoid losing."

"That's the name of the game, Sheriff."

"Not to lose? Hell, that's the name of any game, man—especially this one," the man said, tapping his star.

"I suppose you're right."

"Hell, lose at this game, and you're dead. You wore a star long enough to learn that."

"Longer," Clint said, drinking his beer.

"Why'd you give it up?"

"The star started getting too heavy on my chest."

"I can't believe that."

"I don't mean that it was too heavy for me to carry," Clint said, correcting any misunderstanding the sheriff might have had of his statement. "I meant it was getting too heavy for me to want to carry anymore. There were too many other things that was interfering with the simpler aspects of the job."

"Politics?"

"That was one, all right."

"Don't have that problem here," Smithson said. "Town's too small for anyone with big political ambitions, and nobody ever wants to run against me anyway."

"Hope it stays that way for you."

"It will," the sheriff said with conviction. Clint got the impression that the man would make sure it did.

"I couldn't help noticing your knuckles."

The sheriff looked down at the swollen, scraped knuckles of his left hand and said, "I don't like to use my gun if I don't have to, and my knuckles are plenty big enough for most jobs."

"Bear River Tom Smith," Clint said, evoking the name of the famous lawman who had patrolled the streets of Abilene before Hickok, keeping the peace with his two fists.

"My name is close enough to his for him to have had an effect on me," Smithson agreed. "I figured if it was good enough for him, it was good enough for me."

"He was gunned down, you know."

"But I always keep this handy," Smithson said, tapping the worn Colt in his holster, "just in case—and I know how to use it. I don't like to, but I know how."

"I know just how you feel."

Clint finished his beer and said, "Where's the best place to eat in town?"

"Hotel dining room's not bad," Smithson said, "but let me take you over to the café. Dinner 'll be on me."

"Oh, no—"

"This is my town, Adams," Smithson reminded

him. "You arguing with the law?"

"Sheriff," Clint said, "that's the furthest thing from my mind."

They had dinner at the café, where the sheriff seemed to be not only welcome, but well liked—and Clint, by virtue of being in the sheriff's company, was welcome also.

The food was very good, and the service was even better, partly because the waitress was a pretty, full-bodied woman in her thirties with dark hair, a ready smile, and a charming personality.

"Thanks, Lil," the sheriff said when she brought them a pot of post-dinner coffee. Both men watched her as she walked away, adding a deliberate sway of her full hips for their benefit.

"Pretty," Clint said.

"She is that," the sheriff said. "She's a real woman, Lil is."

"Sounds like you're an admirer of hers."

"If I wasn't married, I might be more than that," Smithson confided. That was news of which Clint was glad to hear, because he was convinced that Lil was a real woman.

"How long you been married?"

"Five years," he said, with a contented look on his face. "Yep, took me awhile before I found the right woman, but when I found her I grabbed her."

"Met her here?"

Smithson shook his head and said, "She was teaching school over at Winslow, in the next county. Gave that up when she married me, even though I said she didn't have to."

"Sounds like you did well."

"I've done real well for myself, Clint," Smithson said, since they'd moved on to a first name basis during dinner. "I've got me a good, steady job and a fine wife. My only regret is that we didn't have no kids, and I think we're too old for that now."

"Are you ever too old?"

"I sure as hell am," Smithson said with conviction. "I'm not too tired to chase desperados around with a posse, but if I had to chase me a toddler around, I'd probably die of exhaustion."

"I doubt that."

"How about you? Ever married, have kids?"

"Never married."

"Ever come close?"

"Once or twice."

"What happened?"

"It's not something I like to talk about."

"Suit yourself," Smithson said with a shrug, unoffended. "Man's got a right to keep his business to himself. What about this man you're chasing? Claims to be kin of yours, doesn't he?"

"Claims to be my son."

"And you say he ain't?"

Clint hesitated, and Smithson stepped in and said, "You don't know, do you?"

"I can't be sure."

"Plowed a lot of fertile fields in your time?" the lawman asked.

Clint only answered him because the man asked the question without a hint of a leer. "I imagine."

He had no way of knowing how fertile they were, but he'd done the plowing, all right.

"I'd hate to have something like that eating at me," Smithson said. "What are you gonna do when you

# HELL WITH A PISTOL 43

catch up to him? The way I hear it, this lad had gone and killed a whole lot of people."

"I've been thinking about that a lot," Clint admitted. "I'll just have to make that decision when the time comes, whether he's my son or not."

"It'll be easier on you if he's not your son."

"Yeah."

The conversation lapsed at that point, and Lil came over to see if they wanted anything else.

"My friend wants some more coffee, Lil," Smithson said, standing up quickly. Clint frowned at him, but the lawman was smiling, and Clint felt he was probably playing matchmaker. "I have to be going."

"Say hello to Karen for me, Tom," Lil said.

"I'll do that . . . and don't let this man pay for anything, hear?"

"I hear."

Smithson leaned over and said in a mock whisper, "He might also need somebody to talk to."

"We can probably take care of that, too," Lil said, smiling. As Smithson made for the door she said to Clint, "I'll get that pot of coffee."

"Will you help me drink it?"

"I'd be glad to."

"It won't get you into any trouble with the boss, will it?"

"I don't think so," she said, grinning, "seeing as how I'm the boss. I'll be right back."

# EIGHT

After a couple of cups of coffee together it became clear to both Clint and Lil that they were attracted to each other, so Clint waited until Lil Roundtree closed her place up and then accepted her invitation to go home with her.

For the first time in a long time, however, Clint went with a woman feeling some sense of trepidation. After all, it had been playing on his mind recently how he had used women in the past and left them, never knowing if he might have left them with a child or not.

Inside Lil's room she turned into his arms and kissed him hungrily, but she sensed something was wrong and easing away, stared at him with concern.

"What's wrong?"

"It's nothing."

"Would you like me to bathe first?" she asked, touching herself. "I must smell like all different kinds of food, not to mention—"

"No, no, it's not that," Clint hurriedly told her, "it's not you at all, Lil."

"Then what is it?" she asked again, frowning. When he didn't answer right away she said, "We could just sit and talk, if you like. I'm a very good listener."

He grinned and said, "All right."

Clint told Lil about John Adams, about his previous successes with women, both before and since his extensive travelling, and about his newfound fears.

"You're worried about how many babies you might have left behind?" Lil asked.

"That's right."

"What about the women?"

"What about them?"

"Well, don't you think those women knew what a chance they were taking?" she asked. "Don't you think I knew what a chance I was taking when I asked you to come home with me tonight?"

"I guess they did."

"So why should you be worried?"

"I don't know."

"Did you make those women feel good?"

"Yes."

"And did you feel good?"

"Yes."

"Then as far as I can see there's no reason for any worries on your part—or on anybody's part," she said with a shrug. "Now, if you're concerned with whether or not you're a father, that's different. But you just can't go back to all the women you've left behind and ask them, can you?"

"Well," he said, feeling a bit sheepish, "there weren't *that* many."

"Well," she said, moving close to him, "this one knows what she wants, Clint, and you don't have to worry about coming back to check on me. All right?"

## HELL WITH A PISTOL

As his answer, he gathered her into his arms and kissed her, and at the touch of her lips all his reservations fell away.

As did their clothes. . .

Her breasts were like fruit blooming in his hands, full and firm, with taut, rigid nipples. Her hands were urgent on his body, grasping his fleshy stalk eagerly, stroking him to an incredible fullness. For the first time since taking out after the elusive John Adams, his mind was completely at ease. He was intent on what he was doing, on the woman in his arms, and not on what he was going to do when he finally caught up to him.

"Come on," she said, pulling him toward the bed, holding onto his hard cock tightly so that he had no choice but to move along with her. "Come to bed."

They fell onto the bed together with him on top. He buried his face between her breasts, licking the perspiration that had gathered there during the day, enjoying the salty taste of her. As he moved onto her nipples she moaned and cupped the back of his head.

"Mmm, yes," she said as he chewed gently. She swore she could feel the sensation all the way down to that place between her legs. She could feel herself growing moist.

Clint moved his hand there, inciting her desire to an even higher plane.

"Oh, God," she whimpered as he slid one finger, and then another inside of her, and found her stiff nub with his thumb. "Oh, Jesus, Clint. . ."

He kissed her, his thumb moving steadily on her trigger, and then she began to move her hips, moaning into his mouth as he brought her to a shattering orgasm.

"More," she said a few moments later.

He moved so that the swollen head of his shaft was

prodding her slick love lips. It was Lil who instigated entry, reaching behind him, grabbing his buttocks and virtually stuffing him inside of her.

"Ah," she said as he entered her to the hilt.

He began to move inside of her, slowly at first, and then with increasing urgency.

"Ooh yes," she said, wrapping her solid thighs around his waist.

He slid his hands beneath her to cup her chunky buttocks and pull her tightly up against him so that not even a breeze could have passed between them.

He began taking her in long, deep strokes, increasing his speed as he went along. To his surprise, the thrust of her hips matched him stroke for stroke, and she grunted with the effort it took.

"Too fast?"

"Never!" she said through clenched teeth.

They continued to pound at each other until the bed actually began to move along the floor.

"What are the people downstairs going to think?" he said aloud.

"God," she cried out, "who cares . . . oh, yes, Clint, don't stop. . ."

Suddenly, her nails were raking his back as another orgasm took hold of her, and when he exploded inside of her, she seemed to writhe even wilder beneath him.

Later he said, "Well, that sure felt good."

"And it's not over yet," she said with a glint in her lovely eyes. "I've got something for you that's not on the menu at the café."

Before he could reply, her face was buried between his legs, and her mouth was eagerly drawing him to full readiness. When she had him standing up straight she took the spongy head between her lips and began to suck on him while stroking the length of him with her hand. Her technique was expert. She was past thirty and had no doubt known some men in her time.

Little by little she successfully took more and more of him into her mouth, until there was barely enough left for her to hold. She moved her hands to cup his heavy sack, caressing his swollen testicles. He reached down to cup her head as she continued to suck on him, fondling his balls, until he erupted, ejaculating into her mouth with such force that, on the heels of his first orgasm, it was almost too painful to bear—almost.

"Feel good?" she asked, after they were quiet for awhile.

"Incredible."

"Yeah," she said, snuggling up against him, "for me too."

He leaned down to kiss her breasts again, and then his lips travelled down her body, over her ribs, the rise of her belly, the tangle of wiry, dark pubic hair. She was wet, and her odor was sharp and tangy. He flicked out his tongue to taste her, then delved deeper with it. She lifted her hips to meet his pressure, moaning.

"God, what are you doing to me?" she said in a hushed, reverent tone.

"Making you feel good," he said, and continued to do just that.

He sucked her, kissed her, plumbed her depths with his tongue as far as he could go, then centered his attentions on her straining clit.

He puckered his lips and sucked at it gently, then swirled his tongue around her. He moved so he could pin her thighs with his elbows, and then began to work on her in earnest.

"Jesus, Clint, that feels . . . oh . . . it feels . . . too . . . good."

"It can't feel *too* good."

"Oh, it does, it does," she said. "Oh, God, it feels so good I don't think I can . . . ohhh . . . can take it . . . don't stop!"

He didn't.

He kept right on going until he could feel her belly trembling with release. For some reason, however, her release didn't come easily. He worked on her until his jaw ached and his tongue ached, but he wouldn't give up.

"Clint—"

"Shhh!"

"Clint, I can't—"

"Lil—"

"God, I can't—" she cried, whipping her head back and forth on the pillow. Her hips were straining against his hold, and he slid his elbows off her thighs so she could raise her butt off the bed.

That finally triggered her, and she came.

Sometime later Clint Adams pushed himself up on to one elbow so that he could look down at Lil Roundtree, who was sleeping.

The moonlight coming through the window was not kind to her. She looked tired, a little drawn, and she might even have been older than he had first thought, but at that moment she was one of the most beautiful women he had ever known.

And then she was awake.

"Why are you staring at me?"

"Thank you, Lil," he said, touching her cheek. "I owe you a lot."

"For what?"

"For giving me one night of peace."

"Is that all this is?" she asked, teasing him. "A night of peace? What about pleasure, love, and affection; what about magic—"

Laughing he said, "Yes, yes, all of that, definitely, but you've given me the first moments of real peace I've had in weeks. For that I owe you a debt—"

She snaked one arm around his neck, pulled him down to her waiting mouth and held him there for a long, long time.

"All you owe me, mister," she said after they broke the kiss, "is the rest of the night. That's all I want from you, Clint Adams."

"You've got it, little lady," he said sincerely. "You've got it."

# NINE

Breakfast in the morning was at the café, on Lil, who cooked it and served it.

"Don't let this go to your head, though," she said with a grin, placing a steaming plate of ham, eggs and potatoes in front of him. "I do it for all the men I sleep with."

"I'll remember that."

"I'll bring the coffee and the biscuits."

While he was finishing up Tom Smithson came in and walked over to his table.

"Join me," he invited the lawman.

"Thanks."

He knew immediately that something was wrong. The gangly lawman looked troubled.

"Anything wrong?" he asked as the sheriff poured himself a cup of coffee.

"Naw, nothing," Smithson answered.

"I want to thank you for introducing me to Lil, Tom," Clint said.

"You got along?"

"Oh, yes."

"That's good," Smithson said, absently sipping at his coffee.

"Listen," he said after a moment, "any idea how much longer you'll be in town?"

Lil had asked him that same question that morning. He gave Smithson the same answer he had given Lil Roundtree.

"I don't know."

"Mmm," Smithson said. The coffee was scalding, but he poured it down like he didn't notice. "I gotta go to work, Clint. I'll see you later."

"Sure, Tom."

He watched the tall lawman walk out, wondering what it was he wanted.

"Problem?"

He looked up and saw Lil standing next to his table, frowning.

"I don't know, Lil," he said. Then, on impulse, he asked, "Tell me about Tom Smithson."

"Tom?" she said, sitting across from him. It was still early, and there was only a couple of other customers in the place. "He's honest, hardworking—"

"Good at his job?"

"Very good."

"What does he have to handle?"

"Not much," she admitted. "Hardwood's not a real lively town. Couple of drunks here and there, but beyond that. . ." she shrugged.

"How long's he been the law here?"

"Years."

"And he's never had to handle anything more than a few drunks?"

# HELL WITH A PISTOL 55

"Oh, about five years back he had a run in with some boys. In fact, he got shot," she said, as if she'd just remembered.

"Bad?"

She shrugged again and said, "He was laid up for a while, but he came back."

"I see. He wasn't married then, was he?"

"Uh, no. That came later."

"Thanks, honey."

"Sure."

Some more customers walked in, and she went to take care of them.

Smithson's past seemed to fit a pattern that Clint knew all too well. During the past five years since he'd been shot, he'd gotten married and hadn't had to handle anything that was very serious.

What would happen if all of a sudden Smithson *did* have to handle something serious?

According to the pattern, he wouldn't look forward to it. In fact, he might even be looking to avoid it.

He might not even be able to handle it at all.

Was that why he wanted to know how long the Gunsmith would be in town?

Clint decided to ask around and see if something was in the air.

Clint spent some time in the saloon talking to people, but nobody seemed to know anything. It was then he decided that maybe the best thing to do was go and see Mrs. Smithson.

Karen Smithson turned out to be a very pretty woman with soft brown hair and a ready smile, which she flashed for Clint when he introduced himself.

"Please, come in," she said, backing away to allow him to do so.

The Smithson house was a small, wooden house with a white picket fence that was in a state of disrepair.

"Tom told me about meeting you. He was very excited about it."

"That was yesterday, Mrs. Smithson."

"Please, call me Karen."

"I'm concerned with what happened between last night and this morning."

"What do you mean?" she asked, her attitude suddenly becoming guarded.

"He was troubled when I saw him this morning," Clint said. "That's not the man I met yesterday."

"You haven't even known him a full day and you saw that?"

"It wasn't hard to see, Karen," he said. "Tell me what's wrong."

She sat down heavily, and her ready smile disappeared.

"I'm terribly worried, Mr. Adams."

"Clint."

"Something terrible is going to happen."

"Tell me about it."

"Something happened to Tom before we were married."

"He was shot."

"You know about that?"

"Yes."

"Well, he put some men in jail back then and . . . and he got a telegram yesterday. I showed it to him last night."

"They're out?"

"Yes."

"Who was the telegram from?" he asked. "The prison? To warn him?"

She shook her head.

"It was from Casey Turner."

"Turner? Who's he? The warden?"

"No," she said, looking up at him. "Casey Turner is one of the men Tom put in jail."

"*He* sent Tom a telegram?" Clint asked in disbelief.

"Tom can't handle men like that anymore, Clint," Karen said. "I love him, but he's not the man he was five years ago, and Turner isn't coming to town alone."

"And Tom feels he has to face them?"

"Tom has to face Turner!" Karen said bitterly. "That's what he says!"

"What's so special about Casey Turner?"

"Turner's the man who shot Tom five years ago," Karen Smithson said, "and now he's coming back to finish the job!"

# TEN

"Hello, Tom," Clint said, entering the sheriff's office without knocking.

"Clint," Tom Smithson said, looking up from behind his desk.

"Got a few minutes?"

"Sure," Smithson said, gesturing, "take a seat."

Clint sat down opposite the lawman and regarded him silently for a few moments. Smithson looked totally different from the man he'd met the day before. He looked pale, and he obviously had not slept very well that night.

"What's on your mind?" Smithson asked, breaking the silence.

"The same thing that's on yours."

"How's that?"

"I just came from talking with your wife. She told me about Casey Turner."

"She had no right to tell you anything."

"She asked me to help you," Clint said.

It had been the last thing Karen Smithson said to him before he left the house.

"She had no right to ask."

"Why not?" Clint demanded. "Isn't that what you wanted to do this morning, at the café?"

"I didn't say—"

"You didn't have to, Tom," Clint said, leaning forward in his chair.

Smithson looked undecided about how to answer Clint, and then dry-washed his face with his knobby, knuckled hands.

"I don't know," he said, and then lapsed into silence again.

"Tom—"

"Wait a minute, Clint," Smithson said, holding up one hand. "Just give me a second, will you?"

Clint gave Tom Smithson all the time he needed to compose himself.

"How much do you know?" the lawman finally asked.

"Enough," Clint said, and briefly outlined what he had heard without saying whom he had heard it from.

Tom Smithson looked at his hands, and then held them out to Clint for his inspection. They were not steady.

"I don't have it anymore, Clint," Smithson said. "Five years ago I faced Casey Turner and his boys. I took a bullet, but I arrested them and they went to jail. Now Casey's out, and he's coming back—and look at my hands."

Clint remained silent because he knew Smithson had more to say.

"Since then, I haven't had to deal with anything more dangerous than an angry drunk, and I handle those with my hands. These hands," he said, thrusting his trembling hands forward. "Do you think these hands would hold a gun now, Clint?"

"I don't know, Tom," Clint replied. "Do you?"

"I don't know either."

"Will you stay to find out?"

"Stay?" Smithson asked, puzzled.

"You could leave town," Clint said, "and avoid a confrontation with Turner."

Smithson frowned and said, "Would you believe me if I said that never occurred to me?"

"Yes, but maybe you should think about it now."

Smithson frowned, then shook his head slowly.

"Where would I go?"

"Anywhere."

"And what if Turner kept looking for me?"

"Maybe he wouldn't."

"He would."

"Maybe he'd quit."

"Will you?" Smithson asked. "Will you quit looking for this fella who claims to be your son and kills in your name?"

"No."

"You owe him something, don't you? Whether he's your son or not."

"Yes."

"Well, Casey Turner owes me, and he's not about to let that debt go unpaid. No, if I run from here, I'll just have to keep running, and I ain't about to do that."

"What about your wife?"

"Karen understands."

"Now," Clint said. "But will she understand when you're dead?"

Smithson was unable to answer that question.

"She asked me to help you, Tom."

"She had no right," Smithson said again.

"Maybe not," Clint agreed. "But you do."

Smithson stared at Clint and then said, "I guess you're right."

Leaning forward, the sheriff said, "I know you've got your own business to take care of Clint, but no one in this town is going to stand with me against Turner and however many men he brings with him. I sure could use a deputy."

"I'll stand with you, Tom," Clint said, "but I won't wear a badge."

Smithson frowned at that, and then accepted it without question. He figured Clint had his own reasons.

Clint and Tom Smithson checked out the weapons that the sheriff had in the office, with Clint paying special attention to the lawman's Colt.

"You seem to have taken care of this gun," Clint commented.

"That's because it hasn't been fired in so long," Smithson said, "but that doesn't mean I've forgotten how to care for my weapon."

Clint handed it back and Smithson, eyeing the gun in Clint's holster said, "That's the modified Colt I've heard so much about?"

"That's it."

"Double-action, right?"

"Yes."

"Gives you an edge, doesn't it?"

"Sometimes."

"Guess a fella as fast as you doesn't need an edge, though?"

"You always need an edge of some kind, Tom."

# HELL WITH A PISTOL 63

"Yeah, I guess."

"You must have had one at some time."

"Yeah, I did," Smithson said. "There was a time when I wasn't afraid to die."

"And that's changed."

"Yeah, that's changed."

"Well, I'd say that's a change for the better," the Gunsmith said.

"How's that?"

"Any man who isn't afraid to die is a fool."

"Well, we may both be fools. I don't know how many men Turner is going to bring with him. We may be facing incredible odds."

"It won't be the first time."

"No," Tom Smithson said, "but it might be the last."

The following day a telegram arrived for Sheriff Tom Smithson. He and Clint were in his office when the operator brought it over.

"Who's it from?"

"Lawman friend of mine in the next county," Smithson replied.

"What's he got to say?"

"Turner passed through his town on his way here yesterday."

"Then he'll be here today sometime."

"Right."

"How many men has he got with him?"

"Four."

"Four?" Clint said. "That's not too bad."

"No?" Smithson asked. "Five against two? Those are not great odds, Clint."

"I've seen worse," Clint said. "Consider that five against two could be a lot worse. It could be five against one."

"It still may be."

"What do you mean by that?"

Tom held out the hand that was holding the telegram, and it was trembling.

"I don't know how much help I'll be to you," he said, "and you're the one who's supposed to be helping me."

"You'll be fine when the time comes," Clint assured him, with more confidence than he felt.

"How can you be so sure?"

"Look," Clint said. "You're not going to run, right?"

"Right."

"And you're afraid to die, right?"

"Right."

"And when Turner gets here, if your hands are still trembling like that," Clint said, pointing, "we're both likely to die, right?"

"Uh, right."

"See?"

"See what?"

"When the time comes," Clint said, "you'll be fine—or you'll be dead."

# ELEVEN

Casey Turner signalled his men to stop, and Mike Blessing pulled in alongside him while the other laid back.

"There it is," Blessing said, looking down Hardwood. The town seemed to be in the center of a great dustbowl. "What are we waiting for?"

"Let Smithson wait," Turner said.

Casey Turner was in his thirties, but his five years in prison had not been kind to him. He could just as easily have passed for a much older man.

"You're talking like he knows we're coming."

"He does. I sent him a telegram."

"You sent him—I don't believe it," Blessing said.

Mike Blessing was about twenty-five. His older brother, Dolph Blessing, had been Turner's cellmate. Dolph had assured Casey that when he got out and went back to pay his debt to Sheriff Tom Smithson, a Blessing would be beside him. Since Mike worshipped his older brother, who still had two years to do in prison, he readily agreed to go along and to bring three of his friends. Dolph had assured Turner that whatever men Mike supplied would be capable.

"That's all they'll have to be," Turner had said. He was confident that he could handle Smithson alone. He'd almost killed him five years ago, and now he'd finish the job. All he needed was a little extra backup.

Mike had brought in Jim Campbell, who was his and Dolph's cousin and was pretty handy with a gun; Shep Norton, who was a decent shot with a rifle; and Harry Newbright, who was half Indian and could do some tricks with a blade.

"Did you tell him when you'd be here?" Blessing demanded sarcastically.

"No," Turner said. "Someone else probably did that for me."

"Like who?"

"The sheriff in that last town we stopped in," Turner told Blessing. "He's a friend of Smithson's. I'm sure he sent a telegram after we passed through his town."

"That's just great," Blessing said. "So then he's waiting for us."

"That's right."

"That's crazy."

"It would be if we were to ride in now," Turner said.

Blessing got the idea and said, "But we ain't about to do that, are we?"

"No, Mike, we ain't," Turner said. "Tell the men to dismount and make camp. We're going to let Sheriff Tom Smithson wait a little longer to die."

## HELL WITH A PISTOL

Turner stared down at Hardwood and added, "Let him think on it."

"It's getting late," Tom Smithson said, looking out his office window. "Be dark soon."

"Maybe he intends to come in after dark."

"No," Smithson said, shaking his head. He turned to look at Clint and said, "He's playing it cute. He wants to make me sweat."

"Tomorrow then."

"Yeah, I'd bet on it," the lawman said. "He'd probably like to make me wait longer, but he'll get too impatient for that." Smithson looked out the window again and said, "Yep, tomorrow for sure."

"We been here a long time, Mike," Jim Campbell said to Blessing. "How much longer we gonna wait?"

"As long as he says," Blessing said, gesturing toward Casey Turner.

Turner was sitting with his seventh—or was it his eighth—cup of coffee in his hands, staring down at Hardwood.

"It's his decision," Blessing added, "and his fight."

"So what are we doing here?" Campbell asked.

"We're here because my brother wanted to help Turner," Blessing said. "We're here for Dolph. Don't forget that, Jim."

"All right, take it easy," Campbell said. "The others were asking is all."

"Well, tell them what I told you. We're probably going to spend the night here."

"I'll tell them," Campbell said, "but they ain't gonna like it."

"They don't have to."

In point of fact the other two men did not like it at all, especially Shep Norton.

"If I don't get me a woman soon . . ." he said, shaking his head.

"You'll get a woman after we've finished doing what we came here to do," Campbell said.

As Jim Campbell went back to sit with his cousin, Harry Newbright heard Norton say, "That's easy for you to say."

Newbright was the only man who was aware of Norton leaving for Hardwood after they had all bedded down. But the Indian didn't care what happened because he got paid any way things went, so he went back to sleep.

There was a knock on Clint's door late, as he was getting ready to go to bed.

"Who is it?" he called out.

"Smithson."

Clint crossed to the door and opened it a crack.

"I just heard there's a stranger in town. He rode in late."

"How'd you find out?"

"I put the word out that I should be told if someone showed up late."

"Who let you know? The hotel clerk?"

"No," Smithson said. "Holly McQuinn sent me word that he was at her place."

"Her place?" Clint asked. "A boarding house?"

"Not exactly," Smithson said. "Are you coming?"

"Let me get dressed."

# HELL WITH A PISTOL

Clint closed the door and grabbed his pants from the bedpost.

"You're going to Holly's, huh?" Lil Roundtree said, sitting naked in Clint's bed.

"Yeah, I guess so. What kind of place is it?"

"A place where you'd have to pay to do what we were just about to do."

"A cathouse?" Clint said, sliding his legs into his pants. "In that case you've got nothing to fear. I'll be back real soon."

"You think so?"

"I know so," he said. "Just don't you go away."

"Oh, I won't," she said, lying on her belly so he could see the rise of her chunky buttocks. "I've heard that Holly has some lovely girls in her place, not to mention herself. I want to see you leave all that and come back here to me."

"You'll see it," Clint assured her, strapping on his gunbelt. He moved to the bed to bend and kiss her while sliding his hand over the firm flesh of her buttocks, trailing a finger along the crack between them.

"You can bet on it."

# TWELVE

"He's upstairs with Leila," Holly McQuinn said to Tom Smithson while studying Clint Adams with interest.

Clint could see that Lil was right, at least about Holly McQuinn herself. She was a big breasted, red-haired Irish woman in her mid-thirties, and if he hadn't had Lil waiting for him in his hotel room. . .

"Let's go," Smithson said.

They ascended the stairs to the second floor, and Clint wondered how Tom Smithson knew which room was Leila's. The obvious answer was that in spite of the fact that he had a pretty young wife at home, he'd been to Holly's place before.

"This is it," the lawman said.

"If we don't knock we might catch him with his pants down," Clint pointed out.

"Then by all means," Tom Smithson said, "let's not."

As the sheriff of Hardwood prepared to kick the door in Clint noticed the hand he was holding his gun in.

71

It was rock steady.

Not only did the man in the room have his pants down, he was totally naked, and so was the girl with him. The girl was on the floor in front of the man, who had a handful of her hair.

"Jesus, am I glad to see you, Tom," the girl said. She was a pretty, slender brunette, and her face was twisted in pain. "I thought he was going to pull my hair out."

"You like to be rough with women, friend?" Smithson asked the man.

"What is this?" the man demanded. "I paid for this gal's time."

"Let go of her hair," Clint said.

The man obeyed, and the girl scrambled to her feet. She had a slim, boyish behind and her pert, dark-nippled breasts bobbed in a tantalizing fashion. She was well aware of the fact that three pairs of eyes were watching her closely.

"Get dressed, Leila," Smithson told her. "We're gonna be using your room for a while."

"Do I have to give him his money back?" she asked, pulling her dress back on, giving Clint a frank examination with a saucy grin.

"No."

"What do you mean—" the man demanded but Smithson cut him off curtly.

"You shut up!" Smithson told the man. To Leila he said, "Go on outside, honey."

"She's got my money—"

Smithson cocked his gun and said, "Mister, if you don't shut up, you won't need whores anymore." He looked at Leila then and said, "Pardon, Leila."

"No offense taken, Tom."

## HELL WITH A PISTOL

"Go ahead out now."

But instead of leaving right away the girl backed into Clint and, gazing at him from over her shoulder asked, "Would you help a girl out?"

Clint holstered his gun and fastened her dress for her, brushing her warm flesh with the back of his hand. She bumped him again with her warm buttocks, and he felt himself responding to the contact.

And so did she.

"Thanks," she said and left, pulling the door shut behind her.

"Can I get dressed now?" the naked man asked.

"Hell, no," Clint said.

"Where the fuck is Norton?" Casey Turner demanded.

He was the first to awaken, and when he saw that Norton wasn't around, he bellowed out and started kicking the others awake.

"Come on! Come on, damn it!" he shouted at the others.

"What the—" Campbell said, sitting up and covering his head with his arms.

"Hey!" Newbright said, coming awake.

"What's wrong, Turner?" Mike Blessing asked.

"Norton's gone," Turner said, glaring at the three of them. "Didn't anyone hear him leave?"

"I did."

They all looked over to where Harry Newbright had set up his bedroll.

"What?" Turner said.

"I saw him leave."

Those four words were the most Turner had heard the half-breed string together since they'd met.

"Why didn't you stop him?"

Newbright shrugged.

"A man has a right to go where he pleases," Newbright said.

"You should have stopped him," Turner said. "If he goes to town and ruins this—"

"Ruins what?" Blessing asked, standing up. "Come on, Turner, calm down. You said yourself that Smithson knows you're coming. What could Norton possibly do to ruin this for you?"

Turner glared at Blessing, then Newbright, then backed off without directing the glare at Campbell.

"So there's four of us instead of five," Blessing went on. "You said you didn't need us to handle Smithson anyway. We were just along to keep the rest of the town out of it. We can do that without Norton."

Turner seemed to be calming down, so Blessing kept talking.

"Besides, if Norton's already in town, it may work to our advantage."

"All right," Turner said finally. "Mount up. We're going in."

"How about some coffee first?" Blessing suggested. "Maybe you should calm down first."

"I'm calm," Turner started to shout and then stopped himself. He had not realized it, but he had awakened feeling nervous about facing Tom Smithson after all these years.

"Campbell," he said.

"What?"

"Make some coffee," he instructed the man. "But after that, we're going in."

"Can't we eat something?" Campbell complained.

"After," Turner said. "We'll eat after."

# HELL WITH A PISTOL

He turned his back on them and stared down at the town of Hardwood.

It's time, Smithson, he thought. It's finally time.

Clint and the sheriff had questioned the naked man in Leila's room, and when they failed to get anything more than his name out of him, they had allowed him to get dressed so they could take him to jail. Even there, however, no amount of threats had been able to shake anything else loose from him.

"He's a stubborn jasper," Smithson had said, dropping the keys on the desk.

"It doesn't matter," Clint said. "He's behind bars, which gives us one less gun to worry about."

"I guess."

Clint noticed that the sheriff's hands were once again trembling.

"Tom, why don't you go on home to your wife and get some sleep," he suggested. "Turner won't ride into town until tomorrow anyway."

"I couldn't sleep," Smithson said. "You go back to your hotel and do whatever it was you were going to do when I came and got you."

"What's that mean?"

Smithson smiled and said, "You'd better get back to your room and find out."

Clint laughed and headed for the door, but when he glanced back at Smithson he caught the man studying his trembling hands. It seemed as if the man was fine while the action was going on, when there was no time to think, but before and after was another story.

"Relax, Tom," he said. "Norton's taste for women may have just given us the edge we need."

"What do you mean?"

"It's four against two, now," Clint said. "Two to one odds. Those are better than any lawman could hope for, aren't they?"

# THIRTEEN

Clint went back to his hotel room feeling more like sleep than sex, but seeing Lil curled up in his bed changed that in a hurry.

The sheet was only covering her thighs and legs, and she was on her belly so that he had a clear view of the smooth line of her back as it extended down to the muscular rise of her smooth buttocks. He wished that he could have seen her ten years ago, but she was still quite a sight now.

He unbuckled his gunbelt and hung it on the back of a chair, then undressed to join her in bed.

Lying next to her, he ran his hand over the ample orbs of her ass and up her back to massage her shoulders gently. She moaned and wiggled her butt, then turned onto her right side a bit, presenting him with her left breast. He covered it with his hand, gently running his palm over the nipple until it hardened, and then taking it between his thumb and forefinger and rolling it around before tweaking it.

"Um," she said, reaching down between his legs and grabbing hold. She was either still asleep or wanted him to believe she was. Either way, he decided to play the game.

Sliding his other hand beneath her he gently rolled her onto her back so that he could work on both of her breasts. Licking them, sucking the nipples furiously, he slid his hand down over her belly until it was nestled between her legs.

Finally, he threw one leg over her and straddled her, working on her breasts that way, and then working his way down until his nose was pressed up against her moist mound. He flicked out his tongue and licked her until her behind was grinding into the sheet, and her hands were tangled in his hair, holding him tightly in place.

He slid his tongue up along her moist lips until he found her stiffened clit and then fastened his lips on it.

"You bastard!" she whispered, tugging on his hair to bring him up to her and abandoning any pretense of being asleep.

His rigid cock slid into her easily. She had her arms and legs wrapped around him and was rotating her hips happily. This time he let her control the tempo, getting as much pleasure as she needed, the way she needed it, until she reached her peak with a loud cry, and pumped at him furiously until he was emptying himself inside of her.

"How was Holly's?" Lil asked as she rested against Clint's chest.

"Interesting," he told her, "but no fun."

"What's going on, Clint?" she asked now, wondering what was on Clint's mind besides her.

"Why do you ask?"

"I'm curious about why Tom Smithson would come to your room and drag you to Holly's with him."

"I've agreed to help him out."

"You're his deputy?"

"No, but I'm helping him."

"With Casey Turner?"

He looked at her in surprise and asked, "How do you know about that?"

"Most of the town knows about it."

"How?" he asked and then, answering his own question, said, "The telegraph operator."

"He's been talking about it all over town."

"That's fine," Clint said, sitting up in bed, "and none of the fine citizens of this town has come forward to offer to help the sheriff."

"This town is made up of storekeepers and clerks, Clint," Lil told him. "It's not that I'm defending them, but. . ."

"I know," Clint said, thinking about Lancaster, Texas,[11] when he and young Pat Garrett had to stand virtually alone in defense of the town for the same reasons.

"I've been through this before, but this time it's not as bad."

"What do you mean?"

"Apparently Casey Turner's coming to town with only four men to back him up, and we may have one of them in custody already."

"He was at Holly's?"

Clint nodded.

"Well, that's fine, then," she said. "Certainly you—and Tom—can handle four men."

---

[11] *The Gunsmith #18: High Noon at Lancaster*

"You think so?"

"I mean," she said, looking a bit confused, "you are the Gunsmith, after all."

"Sure, that's right," he said sarcastically. "Killing four men should be no problem for me."

"That's not what I meant."

"I know," he said. "Don't worry about it."

"I—I better go," she said. "You'll need at least a few hours sleep."

"That might be best."

He didn't watch her as she dressed. She kissed him goodnight and left.

After she was gone, he scolded himself for the way he'd reacted to her evocation of the name "the Gunsmith". He'd apologize the next time he saw her.

Before drifting off to sleep, he idly wondered where John Adams was and what he was doing through all of this.

# FOURTEEN

John Adams was in Canaan, New Mexico, growing impatient and bored.

His boredom stemmed directly from the town itself. Originally he had thought it the ideal place for him to rest and re-evaluate the way he had been going about his "business" of becoming famous, but he soon decided that he'd made the wrong choice. This town was too quiet for him, and his only choices appeared to be either to leave or liven it up himself.

That was where his impatience came in. He had become tired of waiting for the proper time to approach the Mexican girl, Delores. The way to liven things up was to demonstrate his interest in a way she couldn't possibly fail to notice. He had just about decided that the next time he saw her in the hotel he was going to take her.

He had discovered that she was married to a shopkeeper who was much older than she was, and that she either worked with him in the store or at the hotel. He knew that taking her by force might mean killing her husband afterward, but that was all right with him.

It was just about time for him to get back to work anyway.

The three Soble brothers were also growing bored with the town of Canaan, and they too were looking for a way to change that.

"Let's take this town apart," Charlie suggested.

"That would attract too much attention," Ned said.

"Not if we do it right," Sam Soble said, to the surprise of both his younger brothers.

"You're agreeing with Charlie?" Ned asked while Charlie beamed. Having Sam agree with him was not something that happened often. In fact, he couldn't remember it ever happening at all.

"Hey, the kid can come up with an idea once in a while," Sam said, grinning.

"So we're gonna take the town apart?" Charlie asked, eagerly.

"No," Sam said, surprising his brothers again.

"Then what?" Ned asked, with Charlie nodding behind him.

"I'm getting tired of this town, too," Sam said, "so maybe we should just make it over the way we like it—quietly."

Frank Montana was in much the same situation Clint Adams was in. He was in Prosperity, the last town John Adams had killed a man, waiting for some sign as to where he had gone from there. But Montana was a professional, and to him waiting was just part of the job.

• • •

Delores Rondo was worried.

She had noticed the young gringo watching her ever since he had first arrived in town, and she knew since that day in the hallway of the hotel that he was dangerous, in spite of his youth.

She did not want to tell her husband about the young man, but she was afraid not to.

She did not know what to do.

Dan Rondo was becoming increasingly edgy as the days passed. His feeling that something was going to happen was growing stronger. He was so preoccupied by this feeling of impending danger that he failed to notice that Delores had also become nervous and edgy.

He knew in his heart that before he let anything or anyone hurt his wife, he would strap on his gun again. In light of that possibility, he had taken his gun out and cleaned it well.

It was ready to be used, if the proper circumstances presented themselves.

A sense of impending danger was also present in the town of Hardwood, buried deep inside Karen Smithson, eating away at her to the point where she couldn't sleep.

Was this what it meant to be married to a lawman? She was confused. If her husband surved this, would she ever be able to go through it again?

Tom Smithson tried unsuccessfully to doze in his office. He didn't want to go home because he knew that he and Karen would probably argue. They had argued before about his job, but never like this. Still, they'd never been through this sort of situation until now.

He was wondering the same thing that Karen was. If he survived this encounter it would be with the help of Clint Adams. Help hell, it would be *because* of Clint Adams. But what would happen next time? And, would it be fair to put Karen through it all again?

Perhaps it was time to give this up. He only hoped now that he was thinking this way that there'd be a new sheriff in Hardwood because he resigned—not because he was dead.

"Sun's coming up," Casey Turner said.

"You calmed down?" Blessing asked.

"Yeah, I'm calm," Turner said, staring down at Hardwood, which was just showing signs of waking up. "Let's just go and get it done."

Dolph Blessing had told Mike that all Casey Turner had been living for the past five years was to kill the man who put him inside. Mike wondered what Casey Turner's life would be like after Tom Smithson was dead.

# FIFTEEN

The Gunsmith and Tom Smithson had breakfast together at Lil's café and Clint noticed how drawn, pale, and tired the lawman looked. He was also not eating his breakfast.

"You get any sleep?"

"Later," the sheriff said, "I'll get all the rest I need—one way or another."

"That's a nice thought."

Clint hadn't meant the remark as a criticism, but Tom Smithson took it that way.

Dropping his fork onto his plate with a loud bang he said, "I'll give you a better one. If I come out of today alive, I'm gonna give up this badge. I've had enough of upholding the law. Let somebody else do it from now on."

"I know the feeling."

Smithson studied Clint's face for a few moments and then said, "Yeah, I guess you do."

"Have you told Karen?"

"I haven't seen Karen since yesterday."

"Don't you think you should?"

"She'll only argue with me to leave town."

"I think you should talk to her, Tom," Clint said. "Make sure she stays home until this thing is over. The last thing we want is to have to worry about her when Casey Turner and his men ride into town."

Smithson started and said, "By golly, you're right. I'll go and talk to her now."

"Tell her your decision. It might make the waiting easier for her."

"I'll do it," the other man said, standing up. "Thanks, Clint."

"Get going."

As Smithson left, Lil came over and examined the plate he left behind.

"Something wrong with the food?"

"Nothing at all," Clint said. "The sheriff's just got other things on his mind right now."

"Can't say as I blame him," Lil said. "You ready for some more coffee?"

"Ready and willing."

"I'll get it."

As Lil went to the kitchen Clint cleaned his own plate and then, just so it wouldn't go to waste, switched plates and started eating Tom Smithson's breakfast.

"Is that supposed to make my waiting easier?" Karen Smithson demanded of her husband.

"Karen, honey—"

"Don't, Tom," she said, holding her hand up. "I been wrestling with this all night." Smithson noticed the tired lines on her face. He'd never seen her look so tired.

"Karen, I can't stay to argue—"

"I don't want to argue, Tom," she said. "Since

# HELL WITH A PISTOL 87

you've told me your decision, I'm going to tell you mine. I'm going back to Winslow."

"When?"

"Today."

Smithson was about to argue with her, but thought better of it. If she was in Winslow that would put her even further out of danger. Later, when it was all over, he could ride over there and talk to her.

"Is that what you really want?" he asked.

"No, but it's what I must do. I can't stay here and wait for news that you've been killed. I just can't do that."

"All right."

"Will you come to Winslow with me?" she asked hopefully.

"I can't do that, Karen."

"Why? Because of your stupid pride?"

"Because if I did, Turner would only come to Winslow looking for me. It's got to end here, honey. Don't you see that?"

"No, I don't."

"When this is over, I'll come to Winslow and we'll talk some more."

"If," she said, "if you come to Winslow—"

He took her by the shoulders and said, "I'll be there, honey. Tomorrow, I'll be there."

He tried to kiss her, but she turned her head away. After he had left, she was sorry that she had not kissed him.

Would she ever have another chance?

When Smithson got to his office, he found Clint Adams there waiting for him.

"How'd it go?" Clint asked.

"Not good," he said, and then recounted the conversation he'd had with his wife.

"Well, at least she'll be out of town," Clint said afterward.

"That's the only good part," Smithson agreed, seating himself behind his desk.

Clint went over to the gunrack and idly examined the rifles and shotguns there. He had already checked all of the weapons to be sure that they were all in proper working condition.

"Should one of us stay by the window at all times?" he asked Smithson.

The lawman shook his head and said, "Not necessary. I couldn't find anyone else to stand with us, but the liveryman said he'd let us know when the riders got into town."

"Good enough," Clint said.

Smithson had his hands clasped in front of him in the desk and was staring at them without seeing them. Clint decided that the man's mind would be better put to something other than brooding.

"I think these will suit the situation," Clint said, taking two shotguns down from the gunrack. He walked to the desk and handed one to the sheriff, who laid it across the desktop. "I've checked them out."

"Fine."

"We should be able to handle four or five men with these and our handguns."

"Fine," Smithson said again.

Clint decided to try another tact.

"Want to play cards to pass the time?"

At that Smithson looked up and asked, "What stakes?"

● ● ●

# HELL WITH A PISTOL

Karen Smithson was at the livery stable watching Jake, the liveryman, hook a team to a buggy for her.

"Can't say as I blame you for leaving, Mrs. Smithson," Jake was saying.

"Really?" she answered absently.

"All hell's gonna break out here real soon, and the sheriff sure don't need to worry about you with everything else that's gonna be happening."

Karen had tuned the man out by this time, and when she did not reply, Jake took that as a sign that he should continue droning on.

He stopped in mid-sentence, however, as he led the team to the door for her. Although she had not been paying attention to him, she recognized that he had stopped rather abruptly.

"What is it, Jake?"

"I got to go, Mrs. Smithson," he said hurriedly.

"Why?"

"I got to go and tell the sheriff about this."

As he hurried from the livery she walked to the door and peered out. She could see four men on horseback who had just passed the stable and were going in the direction of Hardwood's main street.

Oh my God, she thought. They're here.

"The stakes don't matter," Clint said, producing a deck of cards he'd gotten from the saloon. "We won't be able to match the stakes we'll be playing for later on anyway."

Recognizing the truth in that remark Smithson shrugged and said, "Deal."

Clint maneuvered his chair around so that his back wasn't to the door, tossed the deck to Smithson and said, "You deal."

"Sure."

He watched carefully as Tom Smithson dealt out five cards to each of them and noticed that the sheriff's hands were nice and steady.

Having taken a shortcut down an alley, Jake burst into the sheriff's office and said, "Riders, Sheriff!"

Smithson put down his full house and asked, "How many, Jake?"

"Four, headin' this way."

"Okay, thanks," the sheriff said, but as Jake turned to leave he called out, "Jake!"

"Yeah?"

"Have you seen my wife this morning?"

"Sure have," the liveryman said. "I just hitched up a buggy for her."

"Okay, thanks."

After Jake left, Clint said, "Well at least Karen is out of danger."

"Yeah," Smithson said, standing up and grabbing his shotgun. "Wish I could say the same for us."

As they rode down the main street, Mike Blessing asked Casey Turner, "How should we let him know we're here? Fire a few shots?"

Turner watched a man leave the sheriff's office and run down the street the other way and said, "That won't be necessary. He already knows."

When Clint and Smithson stepped out of the sheriff's office they saw four men on horseback set up in the center of the street with a horse-length between them.

## HELL WITH A PISTOL 91

"They're too far apart for the scatterguns," Smithson said.

"Not if we each take two," Clint said, but he knew for that to work they'd have to stand far enough away for the buckshot to spread. He hoped that the spread pattern wouldn't be too thin.

"Which one's Turner?"

"Second from the left."

"You want him?"

Clint didn't look at Smithson while he waited for the answer. He was watching the four men.

"Yeah, I want him."

"Okay," Clint said. "Put down the shotgun."

"What? Why?"

"You won't need it."

"Why?"

"Because you just have to worry about Turner," the Gunsmith said, putting down his own shotgun. "I'll take care of the other three."


Karen Smithson watched as Clint and her husband stepped down and moved into the center of the street. She was behind Casey Turner and his men, holding in her hands the rifle she had run home to get.

After Jake left her at the livery, she realized that she wouldn't be able to just go to Winslow and forget about Tom. He was her husband—for better or worse—and she knew that she was going to have to help him.

She didn't know if she would have the nerve to use the rifle, but if she wanted to stay a lawman's wife, she knew she was going to have to try.

● ● ●

"Are you sure?"

"Believe me," Clint Adams said, "I wouldn't say it if I didn't mean it. As far as you're concerned, this is between Casey Turner and you. There's nobody else on the street."

"I don't know if I can do that," Tom Smithson said.

"Tom, believe me, I want to come out of this alive. Just do as I say."

"All right, Clint," Smithson said. "All right."

"Then let's do it."

Together they stepped off the boardwalk into the street.

# SIXTEEN

"It's been a long time, Sheriff," Casey Turner called out.

"Not long enough for me, Turner," Smithson replied. "You and your men didn't just rob a bank five years ago. You killed a teller."

"I didn't kill anyone, Smithson," Turner said. Turner had simply gotten five years, a court of law having found him innocent of murder. Smithson always suspected that the jury had been bought off the murder charge, but he couldn't prove it. "I'm gonna change that now though."

"Are you?"

"That's what I'm here for."

"Turner, why don't you just take these men and ride out of Hardwood," Clint Adams spoke up. "There's no reason for any of you to die." He didn't look at Turner while he spoke, he was too busy watching the other three men. Aside from the obvious one of numbers, he knew he was at a disadvantage because the third man was across the street, to Turner's right. He was going to have to handle the two men in front of him, then fire across Smithson's line of fire to take out the third.

Turner squinted at Clint and asked, "You a deputy or something?"

"Something," Clint said.

"Well, this ain't your fight, mister."

"I'm making it mine."

"Then you'll die along with the sheriff."

"Casey?"

It was Blessing who was on Turner's right and across from the Gunsmith.

"What?"

"I know that man."

"So?"

"I've seen him before."

"So what?"

"Casey, he's the Gunsmith!"

The other two men, Campbell and Newbright, looked over at Blessing, recognizing the name.

"The Gunsmith!" Campbell said. He was standing all the way to Clint's right, while Newbright was the man all the way to the left.

"It doesn't matter who he is," Turner called out.

"Like hell it don't," Campbell said. "I didn't sign on to face the Gunsmith."

"Campbell, you're yellow!" Turner said.

"Maybe," Campbell said, "but at least I'll be alive."

Jim Campbell turned his horse and began riding back the way he came.

"Blessing?" Turner said, looking over at Mike Blessing.

"I'm with you, Turner."

"You told me you'd have men who weren't afraid."

"You still got Newbright and me."

Turner looked over at Newbright, who hadn't spoken up to that point.

"What about it?"

The half-breed's dark eyes studied everyone on the street—Smithson, Turner, Blessing, back at the retreating Campbell, and then finally the Gunsmith.

"Sorry," he said, and turned his horse to follow Jim Campbell.

Well, Clint thought, the odds were evening out now.

"Two against two," Clint called out. "Don't you like those odds, Turner?"

"Campbell!" Turner shouted. "Newbright, you half-breed bastard! Come back!"

"Come on, Turner," Smithson called, taking advantage of the situation. "Let's get it over with."

Turner looked at Smithson, then said to Blessing, "All right, then. You take the other one, Mike. I'll take care of Smithson."

"Me?" Blessing said, looking less than confident. "Draw on the Gunsmith? I'm not that much of a fool, Turner."

"Your brother said you'd help me!"

"Against Smithson, yeah, I would," Blessing said. "But not against the Gunsmith. I'm leaving, Turner, and if you're smart you'll come with me."

"No!" Turner yelled, glaring at Smithson with hatred burning in his eyes. "I came here to kill him, and I'm going to do it!"

"Back off, Blessing," Clint said, "while you've got the time."

"I'm sorry, Turner," Blessing said, shaking his head. He pulled his horse around to follow the other two men.

"You're a coward, Blessing!" Turner screamed, his rage suffusing his face with blood until it almost glowed. "A damned coward!"

As Mike Blessing rode out of town, Casey Turner turned back to face Tom Smithson and Clint Adams—alone.

Karen Smithson, crouched out of sight behind a pile of boxes, was confused. She didn't know what was going on, except that three of the men who had ridden *into* town had now turned around and rode past her, *out* of town. Now there was only the man she assumed was Casey Turner to face Tom and Clint Adams. Holding onto the rifle tightly she decided that she had to get closer to hear what was being said.

Was it possible that it was over, without a shot being fired?

She fervently hoped so.

"Well?" Casey Turner asked. "Which one of you is first?"

"What makes you think we have any intentions of going one at a time?" Clint asked.

"You can't expect me to draw on both of you," Turner said indignantly.

"Why not?" Clint asked. "Didn't you expect us to draw on you when there were four of you?"

"Look, Adams, just let me take care of Smithson. It's not your fight."

"Turner—" Clint started, but Smithson cut him off.

"Clint, let me handle this," Smithson said. "I

needed your help when there were four of them, but now it's just Turner and me."

Clint looked over at the lawman, saw that he was determined, and then said, "All right, Tom." He looked at Turner again and said, "Get down off your horse, Turner."

"What?"

"You heard me," Clint said, "step down or go for your gun now."

Turner didn't seem quite as confident as he had when he'd first ridden into town. He glanced at both of them before slowly stepping down from his horse, as if he expected them to shoot him before his foot touched the ground.

Clint stepped forward, took hold of the horse's reins, and then said, "All right, it's all yours, gentlemen. Tom, don't forget we're supposed to have dinner together tonight."

"I'll be there," Smithson said.

Clint nodded with more confidence than he felt and walked the horse to a hitching post where he stood watch. As much as he hated to let it go on, this was the only way this thing between the two men would be resolved.

"Clint."

He turned his head to his left and saw Karen Smithson, holding a rifle.

"Karen, what are you doing here?"

She went over to stand by him, staring out at the two men in the street.

"Aren't you going to stop them?"

"I don't think I can, Karen," he said. "This has to be settled between the two of them."

"But Tom might be killed," she said anxiously.

"Karen—"

"I can't just stand by—" she said and abruptly raised the rifle.

"Karen, don't!" Clint said, grabbing for the gun.

"Well, what about it, Casey?" Tom Smithson asked. He had no idea what was going on anywhere but on the street as he kept his eyes glued to Turner.

"This is it, Smithson."

"Sure it is," Smithson said. "You've done your five years, Casey, and now you're out. Is this going to be worth it?"

"It will be when you're dead."

"And what if it's the other way around?"

"It won't be."

"It could be, Casey," Smithson said. "Take a couple of seconds and think about it."

Turner did just that, and after a few seconds the look on his face changed, and Smithson thought that maybe this thing *would* be resolved without someone dying.

That's when they heard the shot.

As Karen was trying to point the rifle at Casey Turner, Clint grabbed for it. As his hand came in contact with it, it went off.

The bullet went wild.

As the shot sounded, Casey Turner thought that he'd been tricked. His hand flashed for his gun as—.

Tom Smithson shouted, "Casey, no!" and drew his own weapon in self-defense.

Clint, having wrested the rifle from Karen's grasp,

watched as both men drew their guns in response to the harmless shot from the rifle.

Turner had drawn his gun and was undecided about which way to turn, toward Smithson or the shot.

Tom Smithson had his gun trained on Casey Turner but, seeing the man's indecision, did not fire.

"It's over!" Clint called out.

Both men looked at him, still holding their guns out.

"That shot was accidental, but it should have been enough for you two to start shooting," Clint said, moving toward them with the horse's reins in one hand and the rifle in the other.

Smithson and Turner looked at each other, and then back at Clint.

"Neither one of you fired," Clint went on, "so this little showdown is over. It's finished."

To Clint's surprise, Turner was the first one to holster his weapon, followed immediately by Smithson.

"Turner?" Clint said, holding out the reins to his horse.

Turner looked at Smithson, then took the reins from Clint.

"All right," he said, looking at the man he had come to kill. "All right, it's over."

Casey Turner mounted up and rode out of town without looking back.

# SEVENTEEN

By this time the Soble brothers had virtually taken over the town of Canaan.

They had imprisoned the sheriff in his own jail, and Sam had appointed himself sheriff. Ned and Charlie were his deputies.

They had taken over the bank—which had very few assets anyway—and were refusing to allow any further transactions, unless they were deposits.

They had taken over the livery and were renting people their own horses. In the hotel, they were renting rooms for double the price.

They had taken over the saloon, virtually using it as a headquarters.

No one in town had the courage or the inclination to stand up against them.

And that included John Adams.

"Aren't you supposed to be working at the hotel today?" Dan Rondo asked his wife, Delores.

"Uh, I'm not going today," she said evasively.

"Why?" he asked. "Is it because of those three men."

It wasn't, but Delores said, "Yes."

Rondo walked over to her and put his hands on her shoulders.

"Don't worry about them, Delores," he told her. "I know their type. They'll get tired soon and leave, and everything will be back to normal."

She frowned, wondering where her husband could have met such men before, but she was glad that the conversation had been steered to them. She didn't want to tell Dan why she was really avoiding the hotel.

It had happened several days before, while she had been cleaning room in the hotel. She had not been in that young man's room, but when the door closed behind her she was not surprised to turn and find herself facing him.

"Hello," he said, amiably, yet the look in his eyes frightened her.

"I—must work."

He moved toward her, and she backed away. However, the back of her knees struck the bed and she had to stop—or lie across it.

"Are you afraid of me?" he asked.

"No," she said, too quickly to be convincing.

He was as tall as Dan, but thinner. Still, his hands were strong as they gripped her shoulders, which were bare because she was wearing a peasant blouse.

"Please—"

"Please what?" he asked. He slid his hands from her shoulders and cupped her large breasts through the fabric of the blouse.

She caught her breath and said again, "Please!"

# HELL WITH A PISTOL 103

"Please . . . what?" he asked again. With a swift movement he pulled the peasant blouse down in front, baring her breasts without tearing the material. This time it was *he* who caught *his* breath.

The flesh of her breasts was smooth and pale, and her nipples were large and dark brown. He took one nipple between his fingers and tweaked it, then quickly bent and captured it with his mouth.

"Oh, no!" she cried. Her knees bent as she fought to escape, and she fell back onto the bed. He fell with her, but she managed to twist out of the way before he could fall on her and fled from the room.

She had not been back to the hotel since, but she knew that the time would come when she would have to face the young man again. If she could only make him leave her alone without Dan finding out!

John Adams was also thinking about that day in the hotel. He had spotted her going into a room down the hall from him, and when he saw that she had left the door open, he seized the opportunity.

He could still taste her, still feel her large, hard nipple against his tongue. He was convinced that she had run from him because she was excited by him, and he figured that she wouldn't be able to fight her feelings for very long.

He wanted her as he had wanted no other woman during his relatively short life. For someone so young, he prided himself on his past success with women of all ages, but this one excited him like no other.

Maybe this was the day he should just go up to her and take her—but first, he wanted a drink.

During the time since the Soble boys had taken over

Canaan, John Adams had had very little contact with them. He didn't feel there was any reason to. What they were doing to the town was none of his business. As long as they didn't cross him, he was satisfied to let them go about their business.

He went to the saloon and saw the youngest one, Charlie Soble, behind the bar.

Charlie saw the man walk in, the one who was about his age. He knew that he was also a stranger in town.

"Give me a beer," John Adams said. His mind was on Delores so he didn't notice the look that came over Charlie Soble's face.

"Sure," Charlie said.

He drew the beer, brought it over and set it down in front of Adams.

"Thanks."

As Adams reached for it, Charlie put his hand over the top.

"That'll be a dollar."

"What?"

"I said a dollar."

"For a beer?" John Adams asked. "What's it made out of—gold?"

"That's the price, fella," Charlie said. "Take it or leave it."

John Adams suddenly wanted that beer very much.

"Take your hand off my drink."

Charlie suddenly became less cocky, because the voice he was hearing did not seem to be coming from the young man standing before him. It was too deadly.

Still, he couldn't back down. Sam wouldn't stand for it if he backed down.

"Pay for it and I will."

## HELL WITH A PISTOL 105

John Adams took hold of the mug by the handle with his left hand and pulled on it gently. There were several other men in the saloon, but none of them noticed anything going on.

When the mug didn't move, Adams said, "Friend, if you want to live beyond the next ten seconds, you'll let go of my beer."

"I'll tell you what," Charlie Soble said. "Give me two bits, and we'll call it square."

"I'm not paying you anything," Adams said, "for this or any other beer."

"Hey—"

"From now on, my drinks are on the house."

"I can't do that," Charlie said. "My brothers—"

"You tell your brothers I said so."

"Look, friend—"

Adams put his right hand against Charlie's chest and shoved, pushing the man away from the bar and into a shelf of bottles. When several of the bottles struck the floor and shattered, everyone else in the place looked up.

Charlie straightened up and his hand was poised over his gun.

"Go ahead," John Adams said with his beer now in his right hand. "Go for it."

Seeing the beer mug in the man's gun hand, Charlie did.

Sam and Ned Soble were on their way to the saloon when they heard the shot.

"Charlie's in there," Ned said, and they both rushed inside.

"Charlie!" Sam shouted.

There were some men standing together against the wall opposite the bar, and there was one man standing right at the bar.

"Where's our brother?" Ned demanded.

"He's behind the bar," the man replied.

Sam jerked his head at Ned, who ran around behind the bar to check.

"Damn!" he shouted when he saw his brother's body. There was a bullet hole in his forehead, and a red line of blood had traced itself down his nose, mouth, and chin and ended in the hollow of his throat.

"Ned!"

"He's dead, Sam!"

Ned looked at Sam aghast, and Sam looked at the man who was leaning against the bar, sipping his beer.

"You kill him?"

"That I did," John Adams said. He felt good, and he could see that in a minute or so he'd be feeling three times as good.

That was how John Adams became the "Hero of Canaan."

# EIGHTEEN

"You heard?"

The question was coming from Tom Smithson and directed to Clint Adams across a table at Lil's café.

"I heard enough to know that this is my last meal in Hardwood."

"Sounds like the town of Canaan had some excitement."

"And if I can get there in time," Clint said, pouring himself what would be his last cup of Lil Roundtree's coffee, "I might just get in on some of it."

"Well, can't say you ain't had your fair share of it here."

It was then that Clint noticed that Tom Smithson was not wearing a badge.

"Gave it up?" he asked, gesturing with his cup.

Smithson looked down at his shirt and said, "Yeah, I did. Seeing what my job drove Karen to last week made up my mind for me, Clint."

It had been a quiet week since the one-shot showdown in the streets of Hardwood. Clint knew that during that time Tom had been trying to make his decision, and he felt that his friend had made the right decision, for himself and his wife.

"You going to stay on in Hardwood?" Clint asked.

"We haven't decided that yet," Smithson replied, "but whether we go or stay, I'll tell you one thing. My life is going to be very different from now on."

That's what Clint had thought about his life when he gave up his badge, but he still kept getting mixed up in one scrape after another, whether they were his business or not, as the recent difficulties in Hardwood had shown.

Then, as if to illustrate that Tom Smithson would probably experience the same difficulties, he asked Clint, "You gonna need any help in Canaan?"

"I think I'll be able to handle it."

"Well," Smithson said, standing up, "if you need me you'll be able to find me here for a while at least. Lord knows I owe you that much."

"You don't owe me nything, Tom," Clint said. "You just be happy and make that wife of yours happy."

"I'm gonna give it my best shot."

They shook hands, and Clint watched the tall, lanky ex-lawman leave.

Clint's week had been spent pleasantly with Lil, and in fact they were together when Clint heard about the triple killing in Canaan.

"Where's Canaan?" he'd asked her.

"A day's ride south," she'd told him, and he'd laughed at the irony of it.

# HELL WITH A PISTOL

All this time there'd been one day separating him and his self-proclaimed son.

Well, he was going to close that distance damn fast. He only hoped it would be fast enough.

# NINETEEN

John Adams' attitude had changed toward the town of Canaan.

Following the deaths of the three Soble brothers the mayor of Canaan and its town council put the town at John Adams' disposal.

He was not to be charged at all for his hotel room during his stay; he would not be charged for any items in any of the town's stores; his meals would be free, as would his drinks.

It took some time for the news of the shooting to get around, and it was at least three days before the town of Hardwood got the news. However, during those two days some people in the town started to think that maybe this special treatment had been a mistake.

One of the people was Dan Rondo.

Rondo watched as John Adams came out of the gunshop across the street carrying a new rifle. He was sure that the young man had not paid for it, as he had not paid for anything he'd taken during the past two days. So far, he had not entered Rondo's general store, and Rondo still didn't know what he'd do if he did.

He certainly had no intentions of turning anything in the store over to him for free. Business was hard enough in a small town like Canaan. What would happen if he started giving items away for nothing?

Dan Rondo also knew what was going to happen, even if no one else in town did. He'd seen it happen before with young men who had suddenly become "heroes." As the days went by it was going to become harder and harder for the town of Canaan to satisfy John Adams.

He hoped that Adams would lose interest in Canaan and leave before that time came.

Delores Rondo also recognized how dangerous Canaan's hero worship of John Adams could become.

Delores was no fool. She wondered how long it would be before John Adams would demand her favors as freely as he was demanding everything else in town.

When the light knock sounded on John Adams' door he knew who it was.

He opened the door and let the girl in. She wasn't much more than a girl, but she was pretty, with long blonde hair and small, firm breasts. The first time he'd seen her, he knew that she'd end up in his bed, and she came much easier than Delores would.

"I'm here," she said, looking coy.

He slapped her.

"I didn't give you permission to speak."

She started to speak again, then thought better of it. She wondered why he was acting so strangely.

"That's fine," he said, reaching out. She flinched but relaxed slightly as he simply stroked her hair.

"Now, get down on your knees."

Her eyebrows went up, and she opened her mouth.

He grabbed her shoulders and forced her to her knees. She cried out, but was careful not to speak.

Adams undid the belt on his pants and dropped them around his ankles. He wore nothing else underneath and her eyes widened when his thickened penis came into sight.

"I want you to suck it!" he commanded.

The girl, whose name was Helen Blake, stared at him in horror. She had never done such a thing before and now realized what a mistake she had made by first flirting with this young man and then agreeing to come to his room. She'd thought it would be fun and exciting, but she had never expected this!

"Didn't you hear me?" Adams shouted.

The girl opened her mouth to reply, but he quickly reached forward, grasped the back of her head with both hands and forced his penis between her lips. She gagged and attempted to pull away, but the pressure of his hands would not allow her to do so. She finally began to suck on him, recognizing that this was her only way out.

She was inexpert at what she was doing, but Adams used his hands to show her the right tempo, and soon he was able to remove his hands. The girl continued to suck, fearing what would happen if she stopped.

"This is just the beginning, honey," he told her, enjoying the sucking noises she was making and the sensations she was causing. "We are gonna have us a night!"

Helen Blake closed her eyes and joined Dan and Delores Rondo as a person who suddenly realized what Canaan had done by choosing to call this man their hero.

Watching the girl's bobbing head, Adams chuckled

softly to himself. John Adams wondered what the mayor of Canaan would think if he knew what the "Hero of Canaan" was doing with his sweet daughter.

# TWENTY

When Clint Adams first rode into the town of Canaan, he could literally feel the tension in the air. For a town that had just recently gotten out from beneath the thumbs of three vicious men, that was odd.

Clint knew what could happen to a man—especially a young man—if an entire town suddenly enshrined him and made him into a saint. Saints turned into sinners very quickly—especially if the saint was a sinner to begin with.

Canaan, at midday, had all the sings of a town filled with fear.

Dan Rondo was looking out his front window as the lone rider passed by, and he recognized him immediately.

"Dan?" Delores said, coming up from behind him and touching his shoulder. As she did so, she could feel that her husband's muscles were tense and corded.

"Dan, what is it?"

"Uh, nothing, Delores, nothing," he said, tearing

his eyes away from the street to look at her.

"You look pale," she said, touching his face. "Are you all right?"

"I'm fine."

"You look as if you have seen a ghost."

"No," he said. "No ghost. Go back to work, Delores."

"I need your help," she said. "I cannot reach the top shelf."

"All right."

He threw one last look out the window, but the man had passed.

No, he thought, I haven't seen a ghost, but sooner or later Clint Adams is gonna think *he's* seeing one.

Clint left Duke at the livery after getting the liveryman's word he'd take special care of the big black gelding, and then asked about a hotel.

"Ain't got but one," the man said, and gave Clint directions to the Canaan Hotel.

When Clint reached the hotel, he asked the clerk if he had a room available.

"I do, if you do not mind a dirty room," the clerk answered.

"Dirty?"

The clerk smiled a wan smile then and said, "I am sorry. It is not really dirty. I am just upset. We have a girl who comes in and cleans the rooms, and she has not been in for some time."

"Fire her," Clint said.

"She does not work for the hotel," the clerk said. "She comes in to help out."

"Why hasn't she been in?"

The clerk sighed helplessly and said, "I do not

## HELL WITH A PISTOL 117

know, Señor. Please, sign the register. I will give you a very nice room."

"Thanks."

As Clint signed the register he examined it closely but did not see the name Adams. He looked as far back as a few weeks, but all he could find was an unintelligible scrawl some pages back.

"Your key," the man said, and he returned the register and accepted the key.

Clint dropped his gear off in his room, which looked no dirtier than some others he'd been in, and then left to find the saloon. As with the hotel, there was only one, and it was named after the town.

The saloon was curiously empty for that time of the afternoon, which further reinforced what Clint felt about Canaan when he first rode in.

"A beer," Clint told the bartender, who stared at him suspiciously before going off to get it.

When he brought it back, Clint paid for it and said, "Heard you had some excitement in this town."

"Some."

"The way I heard it, it was a lot," Clint said. "Three men being gunned down—that's a lot of excitement, I'd say."

"I guess."

"I'd sure like to meet the man who outdrew the three of them."

"Didn't outdraw three of them."

"He killed three men, didn't he?"

"Yep, but he killed them separate," the man said. He was warming to his subject. "He killed one first— the young one—and then he killed the other two."

"You saw it?"

"Yep."

It had been Clint's experience that people who have witnessed shoot-outs enjoy talking about them, so he asked a question he knew the man would enjoy answering.

"Was he fast?"

"Mister," the bartender said, leaning his large forearms on the bar, "I've seen a lot of moves in my time, but this one . . ." and he shook his head in wonder. Clint put a lot of faith in what he was saying because the man was an old bartender and looked like he'd be hard to impress.

"He was holding a beer mug in his gunhand both times," the man went on, "and he still killed all of them."

"He dropped the mug?" Clint asked carefully.

"He put it down first," the bartender answered, "and never spilt a drop—then took his time and drank the beer after."

"What did the law have to say?"

"The law? Those Soble brothers had locked our sheriff in his own cell—not that he was much of a lawman anyway. And to top it off, everyone called this young fella a hero because those three had taken this town away from us."

"This hero got a name?"

"That's the funny thing," the man replied. "Nobody knows his name."

"Is he still in town?"

"Oh yeah, he's still here," the bartender said with a knowing look on his face. "Would you leave a town where everything was free?"

"Free?"

"That's what the mayor said. 'You won't be charged for anything as long as you're in town,' " the man said. The bartender shook his head and added, "I don't think this kid is ever gonna leave."

"Kid?"

"Can't be more than eighteen."

Everything the man had said led Clint to believe that this was the elusive John Adams he was looking for. But, if it was, why was he keeping the name a secret?

"So if he's still in town, I guess I'll get to meet him," Clint said.

The bartender narrowed his eyes and said, "You ain't a lawman, are you?"

"No."

"A bounty hunter?"

"No."

"Then I'd advise you to stay away from him."

"Why?"

"He's just as soon shoot you as look at you, friend. He's a mean one."

"I thought he was a hero?"

"He ain't no hero, and this town is starting to find that out. He's gonna get tired of Canaan, and when he does he's either gonna leave or—"

The man stopped short and Clint said, "Or what?"

"Mister, I don't even want to think about it."

Another customer straggled in, and the bartender went to take care of him. Clint finished his beer, then set the mug down and looked at it, remembering what the bartender had said.

Put the mug down, didn't spill a drop, and killed two men. He'd never seen anyone do that. Not Hickok, not Earp, not Masterson, not the Irish Gun, Warren Murphy.

That had to be one hell of a move.

# TWENTY-ONE

Dan Rondo tried to set straight in his mind the series of events that had happened over the past few weeks. The arrival of the young hero had gone virtually unnoticed. When the Sobles arrived, Dan had felt that perhaps this was trouble he'd felt brewing. Eventually, the Sobles had proved to be trouble, so much trouble that Dan himself had thought about taking out his gun. The fact that he hadn't used it in over five years had delayed his decision long enough for the "hero" and the Sobles to cross paths.

Then, the "Hero of Canaan" started to prove a problem himself, perhaps even a greater danger than the three brothers had, and once again Dan started to think that maybe he would have to take out his gun in order to preserve what he had built in this small town.

What he had in Canaan was a new life under an assumed name—a *normal* life. He had left behind the life and reputation of Ron Diamond, and he wondered if once again taking out his gun and using it would really destroy all that. At first he didn't think so, because the Sobles were not gunmen—he'd known that as soon as he saw them. But this other man, he was different. Dan saw the way he moved and knew that this man was dangerous with a gun.

If he strapped his gun on again after all this time one of two things would happen. Either he would kill the other man and attract attention—then someone might recognize him, and his new life would be over. Or, the other man would kill him and his past wouldn't matter.

Dan Rondo was not afraid to die, but he was afraid of losing what he had here with Delores.

The appearance of the Gunsmith had virtually sealed Dan Rondo's fate. He knew Clint Adams would recognize him immediately.

A third solution struck him then: to take Delores and leave Canaan, go somewhere else and start over. He wouldn't mind that as long as Delores was with him, but he knew that his wife would ask why. He also knew that she wouldn't want to leave her home or her father. The old man rarely left his room above the store, and without Delores he would be helpless.

Delores wouldn't leave Canaan—not willingly.

Dan stood behind the counter of his store and looked around. This was a failing business, but he had come to Canaan with some money and had immediately deposited it in the bank. He had been using that to create the illusion that the business—and Delores' odd jobs—were supporting them, but soon that would run out, too.

What then?

Dan Rondo's problems were mounting, and it bothered him that the only real solution he could think

# HELL WITH A PISTOL 123

of was to fall back on his past expertise and become the man who had been "dead" for over five years.

Clint held another brief conversation with the bartender and found out that the "Hero of Canaan" usually ended up in the saloon, but that might change because of the man's new living arrangements.

"Where is he staying?"

"He *was* staying in the hotel while he was here."

"And now?"

"Now?" the bartender repeated, shaking his head. "As of yesterday he's staying in the mayor's house."

"With the mayor?"

"The mayor is staying in the hotel."

"How could he allow a thing like—"

"That's not all," the man said, cutting Clint's question off.

"There's more?"

The man nodded and said, "He wouldn't allow the mayor's daughter to move out. She's living there with him."

"And her father allowed that?"

"Mister, you're gonna find out that this man can do anything he wants in this town. Half of the people are still grateful to him for getting rid of the Soble brothers—the half that he hasn't taken anything from yet."

"And the other half?"

"The other half," the bartender said, "is just downright afraid of him."

Clint waited at the saloon until after dark, but the man never showed.

"Leaving?" the bartender asked. "I ain't closing

for another half hour."

"I rode hard getting here," Clint said. "I need a good night's sleep."

"Want me to tell the man you're looking for him?"

"No, don't do that," Clint said. "I'll find him tomorrow myself."

"Haven't changed your mind, eh?"

"I came a long way to see this man," Clint said. "I'm not about to change my mind."

"I wish you luck then, mister," the bartender said. As Clint was leaving he heard him add, "You're gonna need it."

Lying in what used to be the mayor's bed, John Adams ran his hand down the naked back of Helen Blake and over the rise of her flat buttocks. He wondered idly if he should wake her up and fuck her again, but decided against it. He wished she had a better ass, full and rounded like Delores Rondo's was.

What he actually wished was that she *was* Delores Rondo.

He was getting tired of Helen Blake, and he was getting tired of Canaan. Most of all he was getting tired of waiting for Delores Rondo.

It was time for this town to find out the name of their "hero," he thought, and it was time for him to get everything he wanted from this town and then leave it.

Canaan would remember him when he was gone though. They'd remember the name John Adams for a long, long time.

That he swore.

● ● ●

# HELL WITH A PISTOL 125

Frank Montana rode into Canaan after dark. He secured his horse behind the livery and settled down to wait until daylight, when he could look things over.

He had to make sure everything was right before he made his move. That's how he had stayed alive for this long, by not making a move unless the conditions suited him.

And, he had every intention of leaving Canaan alive.

# TWENTY-TWO

Dan Rondo woke that morning with a feeling of dread, a feeling he could not hide from Delores.

"Dan, please," she said as he was dressing. "What is wrong?"

"Nothing."

"Do not tell me it is nothing," she said angrily. She stamped her foot, and he turned to look at her in surprise. He had never seen her display anger before, in spite of her hot Mexican blood.

"I can see it in your eyes, in your face. It has been there for weeks. Tell me!"

She was angry with herself more than with her husband. As much as she wanted to find out what was bothering him all this time, she was afraid to hear what it was.

He turned and put his hands on her shoulders. As always, when he touched her she felt his strength and his warmth flow from his hands into her body.

"How can one so young be so wise?" he asked.

"I love you," she said. "I know when something is bothering you."

"And I know when something is bothering you," he said.

It was true. Of late he had noticed that she was very preoccupied, and it was obvious that she was now avoiding going to work at the hotel.

"I'll make a deal with you, my love. You tell me what's bothering you, and I'll tell you what's bothering me."

Her heart sank. She couldn't tell him, because if she did he would go after the young man and be killed.

"I cannot."

"Well, you let me know when you can."

She was about to speak when a weak, quavering voice called her name from upstairs.

"See to your father, Delores."

"We will talk," she said. Dan nodded and watched her go upstairs.

The feeling of dread grew as he finished dressing.

Someone was going to die today.

When the sun came up and the liveryman opened his doors, Frank Montana put his horse up and asked the man where he could get something to eat.

"There's a café on Main Street."

"Thanks."

"Hey, mister?"

"Yeah?"

"Don't you wanna know where the hotel is?"

Montana shook his head.

"I won't be here long enough to need it."

● ● ●

# HELL WITH A PISTOL

John Adams woke as Helen Blake was trying to slip out of bed without waking him.

"Ouch!" she cried out as he grabbed her by the left arm and twisted it cruelly.

"You'd like me to leave town, wouldn't you?"

"Yes!" she answered immediately, and then ducked, expecting to be slapped.

"All right."

"What?" she asked, surprised he hadn't hit her.

"I said all right, I'll leave."

She gaped at him.

"That's what you want, isn't it?"

"Uh, yes," she stammered, still not sure she was hearing right.

"I want you to get dressed and go tell your father that I'll be leaving soon."

"Soon?" she asked suspiciously.

"Well, tonight or tomorrow," he said. "But, I'd rather not leave in the dark."

"Why don't you leave this morning?"

"Helen," he said, his voice chiding her, "do you want to get rid of me that bad?"

"Yes."

He twisted her arm again, and she gasped in pain.

"Get dressed," he said, releasing her, "and tell your father that John Adams is leaving Canaan."

"John Adams?"

"Yes."

"That's your name?"

"Yes. Do you recognize it?"

"No."

He frowned.

"How about the Gunsmith?"

"I recognize that name," she said, getting up off the bed slowly, expecting him to pull her back at any moment. "He's a famous gunman."

"That's right, and his name is Clint Adams."

"Adams?" she said, pulling her dress on without taking the time to put on any underwear. She wanted to get out of the house as soon as possible. "Like your name?"

"Just like my name."

"She was about to leave when she stopped and asked, "You're related to the Gunsmith?"

"That's right," John Adams said, grinning. "And, be sure you tell your father that I'm the Gunsmith's son, will you? I think this town deserves to know who their hero is."

"I'll tell him," she said and ran from the house.

Her father was not the only one she told either.

# TWENTY-THREE

There was already a man eating in the café when Clint arrived, and they nodded at each other in passing. Clint noticed a man eating eggs and bacon, and the sight of it set his mouth watering.

"What'll you have?" a big man with an apron asked him.

"I'll have what he's having," Clint said.

"That's good," the man said, wiping his hands on his apron, " 'cause that's all I make."

"And coffee."

"Comin' up."

"A pot."

"You got it."

The man brought him a pot of the blackest coffee he'd ever seen.

"How's the coffee?" the man at the other table asked.

"Didn't you have any?"

He shook his head and showed Clint that he was drinking water with his breakfast.

"It's strong," Clint said.

"Uh-huh. Is it any good?"

"It's . . . strong."

"That answers my question."

After that they didn't speak, but Clint noticed the man watching him every so often. He appeared to be a tall, rangy man in his thirties, not unlike Tom Smithson, except that his hands weren't like Smithson's at all. They appeared to handle the eating utensils with a kind of grace.

Clint couldn't see the man's right hip, but wished he could.

That's where the man's gun would be.

Montana was watching the Gunsmith and knew Clint was aware of it. Frank Montana kept a low profile, unlike the Gunsmith, whom he'd recognized as soon as he had walked in the door. The Gunsmith, however, had no idea who he was, and he liked it that way.

When John Adams walked into the café for breakfast there were already two men sitting there, eating. As the owner of the café was serving him the same greasy eggs and bacon that Clint Adams and Frank Montana were eating, someone came running in and blurted out, "Did you hear, Harry?"

"Hear what?"

"The hero," the man said, and he didn't notice Harry's efforts to shut him up, "the hero says he's John Adams, Clint Adams' son."

"Shhh—"

"You know who that is?" the man continued. "He says he's the Gunsmith's—"

"Shut up, Andy!"

## HELL WITH A PISTOL

Andy started, then saw Harry look away and followed his gaze until he was looking at John Adams.

"Oh," he said and backed out of the café quickly.

Harry went into the kitchen and brought out John Adams' coffee.

The news did not elude the Gunsmith, who now knew he was in the same room with John Adams.

He picked up his plate and his coffee, carried them over to the younger man's table and sat down.

"Can I help you?" the other man asked without looking up from his plate.

"Maybe," Clint said. "I understand your name is John Adams."

"That's right."

"I hear you claim to be the son of Clint Adams," Clint continued, "the Gunsmith."

"That's right," John Adams said, still without looking up from his plate. "What's it to you?"

After a moment Clint said, "I'm the Gunsmith." The words didn't come easy.

John Adams finally looked up from his plate across the table at Clint and said, "Hi, Daddy."

# TWENTY-FOUR

"I'll bet you think that's funny," Clint said.

"Nope," John Adams said, directing his attention back to his meal. "I think it's a damned shame."

"What is?"

"That a man would go away and leave his son without a father."

"You still claim you're my son?" Clint asked. "Even to my face?"

"Oh, I would never say anything behind a man's back that I wouldn't say to his face. Would you?"

"What proof can you offer?"

"Is that what you came here for?" John Adams asked, looking up again. "Is that why you tracked me down, to find out if I could prove I was your son?"

"That's one reason."

"What's the other one."

"You're killing people."

"Oh," the younger man said, looking down at his breakfast. "That."

"Yes, that."

"Do you intend to stop me?"

"I don't know."

"Do you think you could?"

"That was never in doubt," Clint said and was satisfied to see that he'd finally said something that affected the young man.

There was nothing physical about the young man that Clint recognized, nothing of himself that he could see. If this was his son, then he looked like his mother.

"What's your mother's name?"

"You mean what *was* my mother's name, don't you, Daddy?"

"Stop calling me that."

"Why, does it bother you?"

"It wouldn't if you had the right," Clint said. "What was your mother's name?" he asked again, using the tense the other man seemed to prefer.

John Adams studied the face of Clint Adams for a few moments before answering. "I don't know if I'll tell you that."

"Why not?"

"That would make it too easy on you. You came a long way for this piece of information. I think I'll just make you wait on it a spell." With that John Adams started to stand up.

"Where are you going?"

"I've got some business with some people in this town, and then I'm leaving."

"We're going to settle this before you leave."

"If I decide to—"

"I've already decided to," Clint said, cutting him off coldly. "We'll settle it, and then we'll discuss whether or not you are going to leave town."

"Is that a threat?"

"Just fact," Clint said. "Don't start anymore trouble in this town, son—" Clint added, and stopped short as he realized what he'd said. He hadn't meant it as a father. He had merely been alluding to the other man's youth.

"Don't come easy, does it . . . Daddy?" John Adams asked, grinning maliciously. "See you later."

"Remember what I said."

"John," the other man said. "My name is John, John Adams."

"You don't come by that name legally," Clint said. "I've never been married." He knew that much at least.

"I know," John said. "That's one of the things that killed my mother after you left—that I couldn't claim your name. But when I got old enough, I decided that I'd go right ahead and do it. Nobody can take it away from me either."

"If you've got a right to it you can keep it, John," Clint said, "but that question still needs to be answered, and it will be before either one of us leaves this town. That much I promise you."

"Your promises ain't worth much," John Adams said, and walked out of the café.

Clint found himself hoping that the young man was not his son.

He didn't like him one bit.

# **TWENTY-FIVE**

John Adams had known all along that eventually he would have to meet up with the Gunsmith. A man like that wouldn't just let some young fella go around claiming to be kin.

So now they'd finally met.

He left the café thinking, so that's him, huh? That's the great man, the legend?

His final reaction was typical for one so arrogant and young: He don't look like much at all.

Frank Montana had witnessed the entire exchange with interest while finishing his own breakfast. He watched the younger man rise and leave, and then saw Clint Adams push his half-eaten breakfast away, stand up and leave also. He appeared to be preoccupied about something.

Things had not seemed to go very well between father and son, he thought. From the way it appeared, one might even save him the trouble of killing the other, and then he'd have only one to deal with.

He wondered which one would come out alive. He had not seen the move of either man, and although the Gunsmith was something of a living legend, there was always the possibility that the younger man would be faster.

Frank Montana decided to find the saloon and spend some time waiting patiently to see what would develop between the Gunsmith and the man who claimed to be his son.

Dan Rondo was standing at the door of his store when John Adams came out of the café. Admitting defeat, he was waiting patiently for the trouble to start, prepared to take whatever action was necessary.

He watched the young man's arrogant stride as he walked down the street. When Rondo looked back at the café, he saw Clint Adams coming out. Since the café was almost directly across the street from his general store, he almost jumped back into the confines of the store, but that might have been just what it would take to attract his attention, so he thought better of it. Perhaps his fears were unfounded; maybe Clint Adams wouldn't recognize him. After all, the years changed a man, and it had been at least eight years since he and Clint Adams had seen each other.

Still, he himself had recognized the Gunsmith immediately.

Nevertheless, he stood his ground, waiting to see if the Gunsmith would even look his way.

If it was going to happen, he thought, then let it happen now.

Clint stepped out of the café and looked up and down the street. He caught sight of John Adams' back as the man went through a doorway further down the street.

Go after him?

No, he decided, not yet. Let him think about their first meeting a while. Maybe after he thought it over, he'd have second thoughts about keeping up his charade.

If it was a charade.

Clint was undecided about which way to go himself, and it was for that reason that his eyes moved up and down the streets. He noticed the man standing in a doorway across the street. He only noticed him peripherally at first and then, when there seemed something familiar about him, stopping to take a better look.

The man's eyes met his, and then he turned and went into his store. The Gunsmith held the image in his mind, seeing a tall, graying man in his mid-to-late forties, apparently a storekeeper—until he examined the figure closer.

It was then that Clint Adams could have sworn he'd just seen a ghost.

Since he didn't believe in ghosts, all that was left for the Gunsmith to do was go across the street and find out the real reason why he thought he'd just seen a man who had been dead for five years.

# TWENTY-SIX

When Clint entered the store, the man was standing behind the counter. His posture said clearly that he was waiting for him. The Gunsmith moved closer, and they regarded each other for a few moments.

"Diamond," Clint finally said as he matched the man with his name. "Ron Diamond."

"Hello, Adams."

It *was* him—the Diamond Gun.

Clint Adams and Ron Diamond had never been friends, but they both bore the same curse: a reputation as a fast gun, along with which came an ill-deserved reputation as a killer.

Oh, there were some men who deserved every aspect of their reputations as gunmen and killers. Bill Wallmann had been one who had developed into that sort of man—although he hadn't started out that way.

Clint had met Ron Diamond eight years ago during a poker game. After the game—from which they had both emerged winners—they'd had dinner together and discovered that they had something in common: they both wished they'd been smart enough when they were younger to avoid becoming "the Gunsmith" and "the Diamond Gun."

That had been the one and only time they'd met, yet they'd spent so much time together that evening that there could be no mistake.

Clint stared at the man for a few seconds more and then said, "You're supposed to be—they said that you were killed, that you died five years ago."

"That's what they said."

Clint rubbed his jaw and said, "You planned it that way, didn't you? You faked your own death."

"That wasn't necessary," Diamond said. "That would have taken a body, and meant killing an innocent man. Despite my reputation, I never did that."

"I know."

Diamond nodded his thanks.

"All it took was a rumor," he went on, "started by me. You know how those things spread."

"I know," Clint said again.

"I kept low and waited, and pretty soon—well, I was dead."

Clint stared at him, shaking his head and said again, "Ron Diamond."

"Around here I'm Dan Rondo, Adams," the man said, "and I'm married. I'd appreciate it if you'd call me that."

"Sure . . . Dan Rondo."

"Is your wife—"

"She's upstairs with her father."

"She doesn't know about your . . . past?"

"No."

"Could we go somewhere for a drink?"

"I gave up drinking when I . . . died," Dan Rondo said, "but I guess we could go out back. No one will hear or see us there."

It didn't escape Clint's notice that Diamond didn't want to be seen with him, and he understood why. The Gunsmith was a link to the Diamond Gun's past.

Clint followed Dan out back after he had locked the front door.

"You did it," Clint said when they were out behind the store in an enclosed alley.

"Did what?"

"What I've often thought about doing," Clint said. "You just took another name and started another life."

"I had to," Dan said. "I was getting too old for all the nonsense, Clint."

The implication of that remark did not escape Clint—though it was no doubt unintended. Five years ago Ron Diamond was the same age that Clint Adams was now.

"I see."

"This was the only way out that I could see. I found this town one day, and the plan formed in my mind."

"So you began planting the rumor that Ron Diamond had died."

"Or been killed," Rondo said, "depending on where you were where you heard the rumor."

"And then you came here."

"I opened this store, met Delores, and the rest is history."

Clint noticed that Dan Rondo was watching him a little anxiously, and he hurriedly told him, "Oh, don't worry about me, Dan. I may be a little envious, but that doesn't mean I'll ruin it for you."

"I appreciate that, Clint. But do you think you could tell me why you're here? I've been sensing something in the air, both before and since the Sobles came to town."

"Well, you haven't lost your instincts," Clint said, and went on to explain about his hunt for John Adams.

"I hadn't heard," Rondo said. "We're a little isolated here."

"I can see that."

"He became a hero pretty quick after he killed the Sobles, and got steadily worse from there."

"Were you ever tempted to take a hand?"

"I'm a little ashamed to say that I wasn't going to unless he got pretty close to home."

"Which he hasn't?"

"Yet."

"I'll have to see that he doesn't."

"I could envy you, you know," Rondo said.

"For what?"

Rondo met his eye and said, "For having a son."

"Ha," Clint said, shaking his head, "not this son."

On the way back through the store they almost collided with Delores Rondo, whose dark, full-bodied beauty brought Clint up short, staring in frank admiration.

"Dan?" she asked, looking at Clint with equally frank curiosity.

"Oh, Delores," Rondo said, casting an anxious glance at Clint, as if to remind him of his promise. "Clint, this is my wife."

"Pleased to meet you," Clint said sincerely.

"Delores, this is an old friend of mine, Clint Adams." In the end, Rondo decided that there was no

# HELL WITH A PISTOL 147

grave danger in telling Delores Clint's real name. She wouldn't recognize it anyway.

"I am happy to meet a friend of Dan's," Delores said with sincerity. "I have often felt that perhaps Dan had not been born until he came to this town."

She was so close to the truth that both men exchanged glances.

"Clint was just leaving, Delores."

"Oh? Are you staying in town long?"

"I have some business to attend to, ma'am," Clint said, "and I'm hoping it won't take too long."

"You must eat with us then."

"I appreciate the offer," Clint said, wondering how Rondo felt about the prospect of sharing a table with someone from his past. "I'll have to let you know."

"Very well."

"I'm just going to let Clint out, Delores."

She nodded and went around behind the counter.

"That's quite a woman," Clint said.

"She's as gentle as a child," Rondo said, and then shaking his head said, "I can't believe my luck."

"Don't question it," Clint said. "Just be grateful for it."

"Believe me," Rondo said, "I am."

Rondo unlocked the door for Clint, but did not step outside with him.

"I wish you luck," Rondo said.

"Thanks, Dan. I should be leaving town soon."

"I hope so," Rondo said, and what he actually meant was that he hoped Clint would be able to ride out of town once he'd finished his business with young John Adams.

Clint nodded and stepped out into the street.

Dan Rondo watched the man from his past as he walked away and wondered if that was where the danger he was dreading would come from. The tension was still there, hanging thickly in the air, cloying, frightening, deadly.

Had Dan Rondo seen the man who was standing in a doorway across the street, he would have revised his thoughts.

Frank Montana had been watching John Adams and Clint Adams earlier, but he was staring now through the doorway of the general store and swore that the man who was now closing the door was very familiar to him.

Clint walked to the saloon and had a momentary second thought about going inside. If John Adams was there, then the younger man might feel that Clint was attempting to force some sort of showdown.

The actual fact of the matter was that Clint Adams wanted a drink, and it was that desire that finally caused him to walk through the batwing doors.

As was his custom, Clint was sitting at a corner table with a beer when he noticed the man he met in the café approach the bar. He got a beer of his own and headed straight for one of the other corner tables, even though there were many other tables available at that early time of the day.

That, added to the fact that the man had paid particular attention to Clint's conversation with John Adams and had followed both of them out of the café that morning, then taken up a position across the street from the general store while Clint spoke with Dan Rondo, all combined to tell Clint that this man was not simply passing through Canaan.

But, who was he after?

John Adams? Ron Diamond?

The Gunsmith himself?

Clint decided to find out the answer without any further hesitation.

# TWENTY-SEVEN

Clint walked over to the stranger's table and stood there until the man looked up.

"Mind if I join you? I mean, since we're both strangers in town."

"Sure," the man said, "why not."

The man had strange eyes, very dark and expressionless. They reminded Clint of Bill Wallmann's eyes just before he had been forced to kill him. Wallmann's mind at that time had been unhinged.

"My name is Clint Adams."

"I know."

"Should I know your name?"

"I don't see why."

"Would I recognize it?"

"You might," the man said. When Clint did not respond, the man said, "I'm Montana."

"Frank Montana."

"That's right."

"I've heard of you."

"I'm flattered."

"Don't be."

It struck Clint that Canaan was in a precariously explosive situation with this many fast guns in town. Historically, although they were something of a fraternity, gunmen were also notoriously competitive. Having this many in one place at one time was dangerous, to say the least.

"Who are you here for, Montana?"

"I'm passing through."

"That's a lie."

Montana grinned without humor and said, "I've been called a liar before. I used to kill people for it."

"Yes," Clint said, "but now you only kill people for money, for the price on their heads."

"Is there a price on your head?"

"Does that mean I'm the one you're after?"

"If you were it wouldn't be for money, would it?"

He wasn't getting any straight answers from the man, but then he hadn't really expected to.

Still, what he'd said was true enough. There was no price on Clint's head; there was also no price on John Adams' head that Clint knew of, and there was certainly no price on Ron Diamond's head.

There was, however, the matter of prestige.

For a killer like Montana, killing someone of the stature of the Gunsmith or the Diamond Gun went beyond the value of money.

"Is there anything else I can do for you?" Montana asked.

"No," Clint said, swirling the remainder of the beer at the bottom of his mug, "but there's something you can do for yourself."

"What's that?"

# HELL WITH A PISTOL 153

Clint stood up, looked down into the man's hard eyes and said, "Stay out of my business and stay out of my way."

"Or what?"

"You're a big boy, Montana," Clint said. "Figure it out for yourself."

John Adams had stopped into the saloon for a free drink, and then he had gone back to his hotel room to pack the things he had left there when he moved into the mayor's house.

In the lobby of the hotel he met the mayor and his daughter, Helen, coming out.

"Mayor Blake," he said. "Helen."

The mayor glared at him, and Helen Blake looked away in shame.

"Oh, come on, Helen," Adams said, "it wasn't all that bad, was it?"

She looked at him and then away quickly. Actually, it *hadn't* been all that bad. Helen Blake was not a promiscuous young woman, and some of the experiences with John Adams had been exciting physically—and that was where most of her shame came from.

Adams left the mayor and his daughter and went to his room. There he stopped for a moment to think about the Gunsmith's reputation. The man was a living legend—as Bill Hickok had been. And yet, Hickok had been killed just like any other man.

The Gunsmith could die too.

Saddlebags packed, John Adams had one thing left to do, and it was something he had been looking forward to since he first arrived in Canaan, something he'd need his hotel room for one more time.

He left the hotel and headed for Delores Rondo's general store.

It was her turn to honor the "Hero of Canaan."

Clint was just coming out of the saloon when he saw John Adams walking up the street in the direction of the general store.

There were a lot of other places he could have been going in that part of town, but Clint had a feeling that things were about to come to a head in Canaan. Ron had a long run in his new identity, but the odds were stacked against its lasting.

Maybe the odds were finally about to catch up to the Diamond Gun.

Delores Rondo was standing at the window when she saw John Adams walking towards the store, and she almost gasped aloud. She looked anxiously behind her where her husband was at the counter helping a customer, and she knew there was no way she'd be able to get him out of the store in time.

Her worst fears were about to be realized.

Clint Adams followed John Adams.

Frank Montana followed Clint Adams.

The thick cloud of danger that Dan Rondo had sensed was not something he imagined. It was real, it was there—and it followed them all. He was watching Charlie Wells, his customer, leave when John Adams passed Charlie on the way in.

Well, Rondo thought, it looks as if things are about to get personal.

# TWENTY-EIGHT

"Hello, Delores," John Adams said, eyeing her up and down.

Delores looked at Dan immediately, and Rondo said, "How do you know my wife?"

Adams looked at Rondo and said, "Your wife and I know each other real well, Mr. Rondo." He paused for effect and then said again, "*Real* well. We met at the hotel."

"The hotel?"

"Only she doesn't come there anymore," Adams went on, "so I came here."

"For what?" Rondo asked.

"For her, of course, old man," Adams said.

Delores looked at Dan and then at John Adams, and fear was plain on her face.

"She's not going anywhere with you."

"Sure she is."

"No," Rondo said, his heart quickening, "she isn't."

"What are you gonna do if I decide to take her, old man?" John Adams demanded.

"I'll stop you."

"You'll try," the other man said, "and then I'll kill you and take her anyway. Why don't you just let her go and stay alive."

"Get out of here."

"I could kill you now and take her."

"I don't have a gun on."

John Adams nodded and said, "Then get one. I'm going to be out in the street. If she comes out, fine. If you come out I'll kill you and come back to get her. The choice is yours," Adams said, starting for the door, then turned and added, "and hers."

On the way out the young gunman passed Clint Adams, giving him a bemused look.

"Dan—" he started, but Rondo held up his hand.

"Wait." He looked at his wife and said, "Delores, is this why you stopped going to the hotel?"

"Yes."

"Because he was bothering you?"

"Yes."

He came around the counter and walked to her, taking her into his arms.

"It's my fault," he said. "I didn't see."

"Dan, you can't go out there," she said into his chest. "He'll kill you."

"Did he do anything to you?"

"He-he grabbed me once," she said. "He-he touched me."

"Then I have to go out."

"Dan—" Clint said again.

"I have to," Rondo said forcefully.

## HELL WITH A PISTOL

"Is Dan Rondo going out there?" Clint asked.

Rondo met Clint's gaze and said, "No."

He released his wife, who stared at him without understanding.

She and Clint watched him walk to a locked feed bin, unlock it and take out a carefully wrapped package. Clint moved in closer as Dan Rondo unwrapped Ron Diamond's gun.

"You've taken care of it."

"Yes," Rondo said, unrolling the gunbelt and wrapping it around his waist.

"You knew this day was coming."

Nodding, Rondo fastened the buckle on his gunbelt and said, "The odds. . ."

"I do not understand," Delores said, approaching her husband. "I never knew you had that."

"This has been part of my life longer than you have, Delores," Rondo said.

"Dan—" Clint began.

"No," Rondo said, "not Dan. Dan Rondo doesn't exist anymore."

"Then it's Diamond."

"Yes," the man said, nodding, "Ron Diamond."

"I don't understand," Delores said again.

"You will, Delores," Diamond said, "you will. I'll explain it to you . . . when I come back."

He started for the door and Clint fell in next to him.

"Ron—"

"I know he might be your son, Clint," Diamond said, "and I'm sorry."

"That's not my concern," Clint said. "Have you fired that thing in five years?"

"No," Diamond said, and looking Clint Adams in

the eye he said, "but you better than anyone should know that killing is not something you forget how to do."

Clint was forced to watch and was of two minds about the outcome. If Diamond killed John Adams, then he would never find out if Adams was indeed his son. Still, he couldn't bring himself to hope that Diamond would be killed just so he could still find out the answer.

"You've got to stop it," Delores said, gripping Clint's left arm.

"I can't."

"Why?"

"Because this has to be settled between the two of them, Delores."

"But my husband does not know how to use a gun," she argued. "He is a storekeeper."

"Dan Rondo was a storekeeper," Clint said, "but Ron Diamond certainly knows how to use a gun."

Diamond was right. Killing a man was not something you forgot how to do.

The weight of the .45 on Ron Diamond's hip was very familiar. Like a man who has lost an arm, he had been feeling the phantom of that weight for the past five years, and now that it was back, it was as if he had never missed it.

As he stepped into the street he looked at John Adams, who was looking at him in surprise.

"You surprise me, old man," he said, "but you're also making me very curious."

"About what?"

"About Delores. I know she's a beautiful woman, but now I also know she's worth dying for—at least to you. That makes me curious about how she'll be—"

"That's enough," Ron Diamond said, stopping in the center of the street. "Let's get this over with. I've got a store to run."

"Confidence," John Adams said, smiling. "I like that."

"You won't for long."

If Ron Diamond needed an edge after five years of inactivity, the cocky, laughing John Adams gave it to him.

"Go ahead, old man," he said, "the first move is yours."

"And the last," Diamond said, reaching for his gun.

The gun leaped into Diamond's hand like an old friend. He fired once, catching John Adams right in the middle of a laugh. Horrified, the young man clutched at his chest and stared at Diamond, as if wondering who the hell he was.

Clint couldn't believe it. He'd never seen the Diamond Gun's move, but he had heard about it, and everything he'd heard was true.

John Adams never had a chance.

# TWENTY-NINE

It had happened so quickly that a crowd had not even had time to form, and soon there was just the body lying in the street.

Back in the store Ron Diamond quickly explained everything to Delores, hoping that she would understand.

"I understand," she said, when he finished, "that we are not truly married."

"Delores—"

Clint heard a voice faintly call her name, and Delores said to Diamond, "I must see to Papa."

She left and Diamond turned his attention to Clint.

"I'm sorry," he said. "You'll never know whether or not he was your son, and I'm sorry for that. If he *was* your son, Clint, then I'm sorry—"

"Stop apologizing," Clint said, interrupting him. "You did what you had to."

"And I may have lost a wife in the process."

"Ron, you must have known that marrying her under a phony name meant you weren't really married."

"I was hoping . . ." Diamond said, and let it go at that.

Clint gestured towards the man's hip and said, "That's some move."

"I had an edge," Diamond said, referring to the fact that John Adams had not taken him seriously and had given him the first move.

"I know a good move when I see one, Ron."

"Yeah, well maybe."

Both men stopped and turned toward the door when they heard footsteps on the boardwalk outside. Clint expected a lawman, but what they got was Frank Montana.

"There's a confused lawman out here in the street," he said, leaning against the door frame. "He's wondering where that body came from."

Clint looked at Ron Diamond, who said, "That'd be Sheriff Joe Lake. I guess I'll have to talk to him."

"Or you could talk to me—Diamond," Frank Montana said.

"Who are you?"

"Frank Montana."

"Montana," Diamond said. "I know that name."

"And I know you," Montana said. "I've been trying to place your face since I first saw you, but I had no problem placing that move of yours. You haven't lost it."

"What can I do for you?"

"Well, right now I'm kind of feeling like a kid in a candy store," Montana said, regarding both men.

"Meaning?"

"Meaning I've got the Gunsmith and the Diamond Gun to pick from, and I'm kind of stuck. Maybe one of you would like to help me out?"

## HELL WITH A PISTOL 163

"How?"

"I'll go out in the street," Montana said, "and one of you come out. Afterward, the other one can come out. See, I'm just undecided about which of you to kill first."

"You're pretty confident."

"And I've seen your move," Diamond said to Montana. "Think about that before you come out."

Montana turned to leave, then stopped and looked back.

"Adams."

"Yeah?"

"I hear that kid was claiming to be your son."

"That's right."

"You think he was?"

"I don't know."

"Well, I do," Montana said. "When you come out into the street, I'll tell you why."

"The truth?"

"You've got my word."

Clint studied the man, then said, "Wait for me."

"I'll clear the street."

Montana left and Diamond said, "I'll go out."

"There's no reason for that."

"Why?"

"He came here looking for me?"

"How do you know that?"

"He knew that John Adams was claiming to be my son," Clint said. "So when he heard he was here, he came also, figuring I'd show up too."

"That doesn't necessarily follow."

"It makes sense to me," Clint said. "Besides, there's no way he knew *you* were here."

"Maybe he was after the kid."

"Only because he knew I would be too," Clint said. "Montana's got a reputation with a gun, Ron, and now he's looking to add mine to his."

Diamond didn't look convinced so Clint said, "There's another thing."

Diamond knew what he meant.

"Do you really think he knows the truth?"

"For some reason," Clint said, "I really think he does."

"And he'll tell you the truth?"

"He gave me his word, and I don't want you killing him before he can tell me."

The truth of the matter was that Clint didn't think Diamond could take Montana, not after a five year layoff. Montana was not an eighteen-year-old kid. He was a seasoned killer.

"All right," Diamond finally agreed. "All right."

"Talk to your wife," Clint said.

"And miss this?"

Diamond walked Clint to the door and then watched as the Gunsmith stepped outside. The street was empty, but this time there were people on each side, watching eagerly. Joe Lake—Canaan's "law"—was nowhere to be seen.

Frank Montana was in the center of the street, standing just in front of John Adams' body, waiting.

# **THIRTY**

The Gunsmith moved out into the center of the street to face Frank Montana. Clint had a ludicrous thought that a lot of money could have been made by announcing that Montana, the Diamond Gun and the Gunsmith would all be in the town of Canaan, New Mexico, at the same time—and then selling tickets!

His friend Bat Masterson would have loved that idea.

Frank Montana was not surprised to see Clint Adams come out of the store first. He'd hedged his bet a bit by announcing that he knew whether or not the dead kid was the Gunsmith's son. That had helped the two men make their decision on who should come out first.

After this Montana would be known as the man who gunned down the Gunsmith *and* the Diamond Gun in the same day.

"All right, Montana," Clint said.

"Oh, that's right," Montana replied, "I made a promise, didn't I?"

"That's right."

"Okay, I'll play," Montana said. "This kid," he said, moving his heel back so that he could nudge the body, "ain't your son at all. His name is Carl Malzberg, and I taught him how to shoot. I guess I didn't teach him well enough, huh?"

"Not well enough to stand up to Ron Diamond," Clint said. "Let me get this straight, Montana, to make sure I understand. You set this up? You gave him the idea of calling himself John Adams and claiming to be my son?"

"Not quite," Montana said. "I taught him to shoot and then we went our separate ways. Later, I heard about what he was doing. That's when I got my idea."

"Which was?"

"To find you through him. I knew once *you* heard about him, you'd track him down."

"And then this would happen."

"Hell, we both know it would have happened sooner or later, Adams. Men like us, we got to end up out on the street, facing each other."

"That's where you're wrong, Montana. We're not alike at all. But you are right about one thing."

"What?"

"Men like you," Clint said, "will always end up in the street—face down."

"Make it happen, Adams," Montana said with a tight grin.

There was one thing John Adams—or Carl Malzberg—didn't learn from Frank Montana, and that was giving away the first move.

Montana went for his gun as soon as the words, "Make it happen," were out of his mouth.

He is good, Clint thought, as he watched the man's hand descend towards his gun.

He was probably almost good enough to have outdrawn Ron Diamond.

Almost.

# THIRTY-ONE

"I missed you," Mary Randall said huskily.

"And I missed you," Clint said.

He put his hands on her shoulders and pulled her to him so he could kiss her. She writhed in his arm, pressing her breasts against his bare skin and rubbing against him, moaning with pleasure.

He lifted her in his arms and carried her to his bed, where he set her down gently. He laid down next to her and began to kiss and nibble her breasts while he stimulated her by placing his hand between her legs, where she was moist and waiting.

"Ooh, yes," she said as he slipped a finger inside of her while sucking on her nipples. "Ooh, God, yes, that's it, Clint, please don't stop!"

He didn't have any intentions of stopping. He loved the way her smooth skin felt against his, the way her breasts tasted, and how her muscles contracted around his fingers.

"Oh," she said, lifting her hips and grinding herself against his hand, "Oh, now Clint, please, I can't wait."

"Neither can I," he said truthfully.

He straddled her so that the tip of his raging erection was prodding her. She lifted her legs around him, pressing her heels against his buttocks, and using the strength of her thighs, pulled him inside of her. Her dark pubic bush rubbed tightly against his equally dark forest of hair.

"Ooh, you're incredible," she moaned, tightening her thighs around him.

He slid his hands beneath her to cup her solid buttocks and pull her tiny body more tightly to him. She might have been tiny, but she had more energy than any two women he'd ever been with.

She bounced and writhed beneath him and eventually she forced him to come at the same time she did.

He didn't mind at all.

"What will happen to Ron Diamond and Delores?" she asked later, after he had explained to her everything that had occured while he was gone—well, almost.

"Ron decided to stay in Canaan with Delores, who agreed to marry him again, this time under his real name. They're going to try and make a go of it there."

"But everyone there knows who he is now, and the story will get around about what happened. What will he do then?"

"I guess he'll have to wait and find out."

"What about Montana?" she asked. "Did you really believe him?"

"Yes, I did."

"Then you have no son," she said, almost sadly.

"Not that I know of," he answered, "but I don't intend to travel into the past to find out." He looked up at the ceiling and said, "If there is a boy or a girl out there somewhere, I hope he or she will grow up without the burden of being known as the son or daughter of the Gunsmith."

# J. R. ROBERTS
# THE GUNSMITH

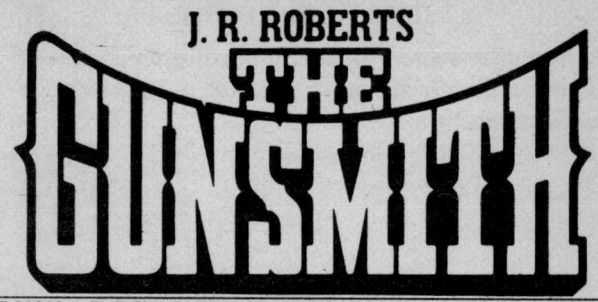

| | | | |
|---|---|---|---|
| ☐ 30929-1 | THE GUNSMITH #20: | THE DODGE CITY GANG | $2.50 |
| ☐ 30910-0 | THE GUNSMITH #21: | SASQUATCH HUNT | $2.50 |
| ☐ 30894-5 | THE GUNSMITH #23: | THE RIVERBOAT GANG | $2.25 |
| ☐ 30895-3 | THE GUNSMITH #24: | KILLER GRIZZLY | $2.50 |
| ☐ 30896-1 | THE GUNSMITH #25: | NORTH OF THE BORDER | $2.50 |
| ☐ 30897-X | THE GUNSMITH #26: | EAGLE'S GAP | $2.50 |
| ☐ 30899-6 | THE GUNSMITH #27: | CHINATOWN HELL | $2.50 |
| ☐ 30900-3 | THE GUNSMITH #28: | THE PANHANDLE SEARCH | $2.50 |
| ☐ 30902-X | THE GUNSMITH #29: | WILDCAT ROUND-UP | $2.50 |
| ☐ 30903-8 | THE GUNSMITH #30: | THE PONDEROSA WAR | $2.50 |
| ☐ 30904-6 | THE GUNSMITH #31: | TROUBLE RIDES A FAST HORSE | $2.50 |
| ☐ 30911-9 | THE GUNSMITH #32: | DYNAMITE JUSTICE | $2.50 |
| ☐ 30912-7 | THE GUNSMITH #33: | THE POSSE | $2.50 |
| ☐ 30913-5 | THE GUNSMITH #34: | NIGHT OF THE GILA | $2.50 |
| ☐ 30914-3 | THE GUNSMITH #35: | THE BOUNTY WOMEN | $2.50 |
| ☐ 30915-1 | THE GUNSMITH #36: | BLACK PEARL SALOON | $2.50 |
| ☐ 30935-6 | THE GUNSMITH #37: | GUNDOWN IN PARADISE | $2.50 |
| ☐ 30936-4 | THE GUNSMITH #38: | KING OF THE BORDER | $2.50 |
| ☐ 30940-2 | THE GUNSMITH #39: | THE EL PASO SALT WAR | $2.50 |
| ☐ 30941-0 | THE GUNSMITH #40: | THE TEN PINES KILLER | $2.50 |
| ☐ 30942-9 | THE GUNSMITH #41: | HELL WITH A PISTOL | $2.50 |

Prices may be slightly higher in Canada.

*Available at your local bookstore or return this form to:*

**C CHARTER BOOKS**
*Book Mailing Service*
P.O. Box 690, Rockville Centre, NY 11571

Please send me the titles checked above. I enclose _____ Include 75¢ for postage and handling if one book is ordered; 25¢ per book for two or more not to exceed $1.75. California, Illinois, New York and Tennessee residents please add sales tax.

NAME _____

ADDRESS _____

CITY _____ STATE/ZIP _____

(allow six weeks for delivery.)

A1/a